Don't bother /

Also by JOHN HERSEY

The Writer's Craft (1974)
The Conspiracy (1972)
Letter to the Alumni (1970)
The Algiers Motel Incident (1968)
Under the Eye of the Storm (1967)
Too Far to Walk (1966)
White Lotus (1965)
Here to Stay (1963)
The Child Buyer (1960)
The War Lover (1959)
A Single Pebble (1956)
The Marmot Drive (1953)
The Wall (1950)
Hiroshima (1946)
A Bell for Adano (1944)
Into the Valley (1943)

These are BORZOI BOOKS
published in New York
by Alfred A. Knopf.

MY

PETITION

FOR

MORE

SPACE

John Hersey

MY PETITION
FOR MORE
SPACE

NEW YORK: ALFRED A. KNOPF

1 9 7 4

This is a BORZOI BOOK
Published by Alfred A. Knopf, Inc.

Copyright © 1974 by John Hersey

Library of Congress Cataloging
in Publication Data
Hersey, John Richard, (Date)
My petition for more space.
I. Title.
PZ3.H4385 MY [PS3515.E7715]
813.5′2   74-9929
ISBN 0-394-49466-0

Manufactured in
the United States of America

Chapter 1 of this book first appeared
in *The Atlantic Monthly*.

PUBLISHED SEPTEMBER 20, 1974
FIRST & SECOND PRINTING BEFORE PUBLICATION

I had not been two years
at the licks before a damned
Yankee came, and settled down
within an hundred miles of me!!
DANIEL BOONE, C. 1801
quoted in Niles' Weekly
Register, *May 17, 1823*

The sight of smoke ten miles
off is provocation to one more
remove from man, one step
deeper into nature. Is it
that he feels that whatever
man may be, man is not the
universe? that glory, beauty,
kindness, are not all engrossed
by him? that as the presence
of man frights birds away,
so, many bird-like thoughts?
HERMAN MELVILLE
The Confidence-Man 1857

We are crowded in, packed in,
now, and human beings must
feel that there is a way
out, and that the intellectual
power and skill of their own
species opens this way.
SAUL BELLOW
Mr. Sammler's Planet 1970

MY

PETITION

FOR

MORE

SPACE

1

THIS MORNING I have some hope of reaching the petition windows.

The tight-packed column of citizens four abreast stretches back along Church Street to the corner of Elm and around toward Orange and out of sight but not imagination. I have been on this line since deep dark, since before five.

I have now come within a couple of hundred yards

of the bureau building. There is less than an hour till I must start for work. This is the sixth day in a row I have tried to make it to the windows.

I felt a flash of line-fear just then, but I am all right now.

As usual at this hour, downtown streets are glutted with busses and cargo conveyors and people shuffling on foot to their jobs. Every square inch of concrete and asphalt is taken up. Wheeled traffic worms along at the stipulated pace. On this sidewalk, at the outer edge of our waitline to the right, one infinity of pedestrians, facing us, inches toward Elm, and another, beyond, toward Chapel. It takes a walker fifteen or twenty minutes to move a single block. This is the familiar suffocating physical crush of the morning hours: breast touches shoulder blade, hip rubs hip, one's shoes are scuffed by others' shoes.

In the street, the busses and cargo vans creep along so close together they almost touch each other. The vans, uniform in design, squarish and chunky, white and immaculate, with no writing on them save for tiny numbers on the operators' doors, look like huge mobile ovens. Across the street, over the tops of these vehicles, I can see the upper part of the wall enclosing the Green. It is a long time since I have stood at the windows in that wall,

looking in: at the empty grass, crosscut and gleaming;
the score of majestic maples, standing apart, whose
leaves turn to each other on stirring air, I think, and
whisper, 'Forest! Forest! Forest, brother leaf!'; the vault-
ing wire cages with great murmurations of sparrows in
them; the three nineteenth-century churches, two built
of red brick and white wood, one of brownish stone, their
spires pointing the way to uninhabited regions above.
The public is not admitted inside the wall. The
Green—green space, a museum of openness. The lines of
citizens waiting on pavements to get to the windows in
that wall, just to gaze at the emptiness within, are the
longest in the whole city. One can only hope to look
through the windows into the Green on a rest day. I have
not attempted it for nearly a year.

Stacked in this waitline, I find myself urged forward
by the hopes of those behind me, so that my body is
pressed full length against that of a young woman who
wears her hair piled upward and at whose nape there are
delicate stray blond curls of an infantile fineness. . . .
*It is strictly forbidden for any person, while in accidental
or formal proximity with any other person, in waitlines,
assemblies, or close passage, to show, offer, signal, or otherwise manifest* . . . What strange murky phrases in
our statutes!—'prurient solicitation,' 'lascivious carriage'

5

. . . It is always the man who is caught, for the obvious reason.

I have come to know this girl. I whisper to her. She turns her head as far as she can and murmurs over her shoulder to me. It is not that we have secrets—we were strangers three hours ago. It is a matter of the psychic abyss between a dialogue of two and communal discussion. We two are in the second row from the right; therefore we have others' ears—and busy mouths—not only in front and behind, but on either side, too. We have tacitly agreed to try to be alone together in this crowd.

To my right is a janitor. To my left, a grandmother, a retired circuitry printer. I have come to know them.

I do not wish to know the man behind me.

There is the siren for eight fifteen. Forty-five minutes left. I must start for my office at nine, or at nine fifteen at the latest, if I am to get there through these teeming streets by eleven, when my shift of writers is due at their desklets.

THE GIRL's dress is blue. She turns her head to the right to murmur something to me. I look at her quarter face slightly from above—cheekbone, little scoop nose, perhaps a large mouth.

6

She has in these three hours already filled me with a feeling of urgency, of a sort which has long been dormant in me. We must get to the windows! I must get to my job!

I whisper, 'Have you seen Zamport's film?' I have some vague idea of asking her to see it with me if she hasn't—even though I already have.

She answers over her right shoulder, 'Just last night.'

'Like it?'

She shrugs. I feel the shrug on my chest. 'I didn't like the scene where they stood in the crowd by the—what do you call it? a hydraulic lift? you know? and she told him about the other guy she'd been seeing? Once she had done that . . .'

From the bits she has let drop about the man she calls Star, or Starr, and from the heat with which she blames herself for the way her relationship with him has turned out, I can understand why this scene upset her. I say, 'That's how those things happen.'

'Mmm-m-m.' Doubtful.

'I mean, we say irrevocable things on the spur of the moment—without thinking.'

She does not answer. She is receptive. I feel it. She seems to be waiting for me to blurt out some big item. I want to. I am tongue-tied.

The main sound is the shuffling of feet. Traffic has

an electric hum, people are talking, there are cracks of laughter. In the distance I *think* I hear the sparrows. The man behind me is a complainer. How tightly squeezed we are! My father told me that early one morning when he was a child he stood on a Cape Cod dune and looked both ways along the sand to the far points where mist dissolved beach and sea into thin air, and there was not a single soul in sight either way! . . . Still, people in this jammed line are willing to risk a lot: to make new acquaintances.

THE REASON I refer to the retired circuitry printer on my left as a grandmother is that she has told me about Robert, her grandson, who is fourteen, who has had a vasectomy and so can be considered a man, and who is one of four hundred pupils in New Haven who have been chosen this year to learn to read. She is proud of him!—even though she regards the skill he has been chosen for as low-grade. She is gray under the eyes, her white hair is unruly, but there is strength in her face, which has in it a trace—dragged long ago through some southeastern European way station—of Mongol or Tartar; a wideness, almond eyes, high cheeks, irrepressible vigor. She could in another century have been a horse-woman, but she has worked at a stamping machine. I like her.

I like less the janitor to my right, because he cranes his neck to hear the whispers I exchange with the girl. He is wearing a clean green coverall zipped up the front, with a gold eagle holding red thunderbolts in its talons embroidered on the left shoulder. He has told us he spends his nights on his hands and knees, scrubbing stairs. He sleeps by day, yawns now. He says to the girl and me, taking away our shared tension about 'irrevo-cable things' said without thought, 'Zamport's an ego-maniac.'

So I suppose he is. Nowadays it takes great vanity, great force of character, a gift for climbing on others' backs, tirelessness, and doubtless a pinch of talent for a man to become famous. To stay famous is almost impossi-ble: there are too many with that climbing gift, as there are too many of every sort. But who wants any more to be famous? I would like to change places with the Mayor of New Haven, who is not particularly famous, whose name I can hardly think of—it is an Italian name again. I want to be he, for he has the priceless right to enter the Green, to mow its grass, to stand alone on the vast lawn.

9

THE GIRL turns her head and asks, 'Where do you live?'

'In the Marinson building. You know, out Whitney.'

'Luck.'

'I don't know. It's modern. But'—I put my mouth almost to her ear and whisper; she can surely feel my breath on her neck—'we're on edge. My petition is for more space.'

'*What?* You're going to harm yourself.'

I am foolish. I know. But I have to try. There is a rumor that they are going to cut down everyone's space. Maximum dimensions now for a single person are eight feet by twelve. What you actually get depends on the building; space is allotted in inverse ratio to the quality of the premises. I myself have seven by eleven—it is said to be fairly desirable housing, the Marinson. A person's space is defined by lines painted on the sleeping-hall floor. One must keep all his belongings within his space; trespassing, except during communal hours, even 'trespassing' by accidental knocking over of possessions, is severely punished. We had a violent fight the other night

10

because a sleeping man, stirring in a dream, stretched his foot across the line into a couple's space while they were—at least they *said* they were—having sexual union. We are told over and over: Survival Is Acceptance. With my petition I may, as the girl says, do myself harm.

If I succeed in reaching the petition windows.

The man behind me barks, 'Move it!'

The bureau building, now tantalizingly close, is a relic kept standing by the Historical Site Preservation Society. A nineteenth-century romanticization of a twelfth-century concept of power, it is stone-built and sparsely adorned, with squinting arches and Romanesque striations, dark-brown and light-brown in color, its walls spalled and pocked and grimed—a fort for men whose trade it is to say: No.

Someone behind us has eaten garlic. Other scents on the morning air: the delicious perfume of fresh-clipped grass from over the wall across the street, and acrid whiffs of synthetic resins from the factories down beyond Wooster Square.

Early-morning mists have given way now, and above the dark roofs of the bureau building white-edged clouds drift in from the Sound, and the brilliant blue interstices pour their reinforcing pigment down on the al-

11

ready blue dress at my chest and wash up by reflection a faint watercolor on the light skin above the collar, a pale, pale sky on the white neck.

The stair mopper suddenly blurts out, 'What was that you were saying?'

He has a dangerous beak of a nose, a double chin, brown hair cut soldier-short, and brown eyes that are much too close together.

The girl quickly says to him, protecting me, 'We were talking about our petitions. What's yours?'

He is gloomy, taciturn. 'Protein allotment.'

I ask, 'What seems to be the problem?'

But some sudden suspicion makes his eyes look even closer together than they are, and he says, 'Forget it.'

Does he feel that too many people are waiting for his answer? With this question on my mind, I myself submit to a new jolt of line-fear. I hold close around me the four who press hard against me in the line: the girl, the retired circuitry printer, this petitioner in the matter of proteins, and the crab behind me. (This last person concerns me in a negative sense only, but he counts as one of the four.) I can cope with these four who touch me. They are distinct—define themselves by their quirks. But the janitor's quick shift of eyes, his tally perhaps of real and potential listeners, together with the fact that the circuitry

12

woman is now telling the person *ahead* of her about Robert, has made me aware that each of the four who touch
me touches either three or four, depending on whether
he stands in an inner or an outer row. My own circle thus
leaps out to include all those who touch the four who
touch me. I must not let myself consider the touchers of
those touchers of my touchers, for like flash-fire the sense
of contact, of being not a separate entity but a fused line-
unit, will carry my selfhood out to the sides of the waitline and crackling along it forward and backward until
my perception of myself is wholly lost in crowd-transcen-
dence. In that lost state I will be nothing but an indistin-
guishable ohm in this vast current of dissatisfaction.

Not that the people in the line melt into an undiffer-
entiated blur. Not at all. The line is a continuum of sharp
particulars. There is a tall black man off to the left and
ahead of us wearing a big knitted red cap with an elon-
gated visor and a huge blue pompon on top. A man somewhere behind me has a constant chest-wracking cough.
A young fellow three away from me thinks himself mod-
ish in a crazy velour coat with a zebra pattern and a
black collar which goes right out to the limits of his
shoulders. There is doubtless a strong personality that
goes with the strong garlic breath. To me, the thought of
being lost in fusion with vivid individualities is far more

13

terrifying than, let us say, facelessness, ego-failure, ano-
mie, exile.

'God damn it, push!' the cactus-hearted man behind
me says. 'I haven't got all day.'

I TIGHTEN MY CIRCLE again; I try to exclude all the
dancing details of the waitline by narrowing my focus to
the stray hairs on the neck in front of me. I whisper, 'The
fellow you spoke of—Starr? What went wrong?'

She murmurs: 'He was so mean. He had a bad mean
streak.' Then at once it seems she feels a need to punish
herself for this judgment. 'I don't know what I did that
was stupid. I'm so stupid sometimes.'

I have seen that she lacks self-confidence. I doubt
that she is unsure of herself because she lost a man; in
fact she probably lost him because of her generosity (to
call unsureness by one of its nicknames).

I will say something to give her confidence—show
her how little I have.

'Have I told you'—we have confided a fair amount to
each other in three and a quarter hours, but I have not
told her this—'that I'm getting a divorce?'

I have surprised her. Her reflex is an odd one. She

14

turns her head to the left for the very first time, I think, all morning, and for the first time I have a three-dimensional sense of her face. Faces are never symmetrical, and she has some kind of bulge above her mouth on this side—gives this profile a more cheerful, even a mischievous, look. Now I can almost imagine looking full-face into her eyes, though I am not sure how wide her face would prove to be.

The grandmother, seeing the girl's face turned toward her for the first time, says, 'Hello, dearie.'

But the girl softly asks a question in answer to my question: 'Is it bad?'

'Pretty bad. We're separated. Lawyers are in it. Been going on six months.'

The grandmother does not wish to be put off, and she asks the girl in a forcing voice, 'What's your petition, honey?'

The girl says, 'I want to change jobs.'

'Why?'

I feel a need to stay in the act, and I say, 'That's the first question she'll get at the windows, for sure.' I have already asked it, and she has told me: Because it takes her four hours through crowded streets to get to work from where she lives, and her petition to change residence has been twice denied.

15

But now she says to the grandmother, 'Because my work doesn't satisfy me. I want to do something that will help other people. I'd like to work, say, at St. Raphael's, or Connecticut Valley, or the Cheshire reform school. Something like that.'

The grandmother says, 'Think they'll care about what satisfies *you*? Hah!'

I am uncomfortable. I do not like this changing of answers. Besides, the girl is not one of the four touching the circuitry printer; the girl is one ahead and to the right of the grandmother. She touches me, and I touch the grandmother, but they do not touch each other. I do not want to be rung in on this second level of touchers. I do not, for example, want to make the acquaintance of the person in front of the grandmother, an elderly man in a shiny black suit—he touches her, she touches me; he touches the girl, she touches me. I have seen his face when he turned his head to speak to the girl, and it reminds me of the face of my father when he was old and sick and had been thinking too much about death. I don't touch him. He doesn't touch me.

The grandmother, however, is really friendly, really meddlesome. My whisper, with my face turned left, about being separated from my wife, has not escaped her. She says to me, 'When I was young I worked in a

16

travel bureau. There was a certain island I used to send people who were lonely off to—you know, marriages breaking up, or maybe just never had had any opportunity for affection. It was my mission, you know, I *thought* it was my mission, to get them all together, so I sent them all down there to this one particular little island. Off Martinique. I never learned whether . . .'

Her eyesight is bad. She has had at least one cataract operation, and she may have glaucoma. Through her thick glasses one sees huge orbs of benignity, generosity, a voracious mothering appetite.

OVER THE GIRL'S shoulder I look at the man in front of her. I have not seen much of his face, although I have noticed that he has turned his head from time to time as he and the girl have exchanged a few sentences. He is wearing a tan whipcord bush jacket, which seems to be well cut and was probably expensive, but he is unshaven, and his hair, balding at the crown, is oily, uncombed; there is something seedy about him. The girl's breasts are nested in the box-pleats of his jacket, her pelvis must press against his buttocks. But he looks the sort of person not to notice pleasure even if it is thrust on him.

17

I test her, whispering, 'What's the petition of the guy ahead of you?'

'I don't know,' she answers. 'I'll ask him.'

In finding out that she has found out very little from him, I have pushed her into finding out more.

She is speaking to him. I see his head quickly turn. He is responsive, his face haggard but mobile. Perhaps he understands pleasure better than I had thought. . . . *It is strictly forbidden* . . . Their exchanges go on longer than necessary. They are having quite a conversation.

Indifferent to the outcome of this chat, I turn to the janitor and say in a loud, unpleasant voice, 'Line's slow this morning.'

Every once in a while, perhaps once a minute, it is possible to shuffle one's foot two or three inches forward. Sometimes, in this shuffling, one winds up a bit off balance, but it does not matter: the crowd-pressure holds you firmly upright. There are sixteen petition windows on the ground floor of the bureau building. You have to realize that each person feels keenly the justice of his request, and when the bureau person behind the bars of the window denies the petition, it is understandable that the petitioner would wish to argue awhile, first in anger or outrage and later perhaps in a whining tone—and all this takes time. Each person wants a fair turn at a win-

18

dow. It takes a few minutes, when you have been waiting
in line, let's say, nearly five hours, to absorb a no. This
time-taking backs up the whole column, which is, I
would estimate, by now, a quarter of a mile long.

At my remark about the slowness of the line, the janitor is suddenly overcome by self-pity. 'I'm not getting
enough to eat,' he says. 'Look. My wife's sick. She's not
right. After work, she'd come back to the sleeping-hall
and Christ, here she'd start yelling at me, throwing junk.
All this stuff would land in other people's space. I had to
take her up to Connecticut Valley. The admissions office,
they said, "Sign here, lady." She says, "What's this?"
They tell her, "This here is a voluntary self-commitment
form." She says, "Up yours, Jack." They say, "You have to
sign it, lady." She jerks her head at me and says, "Get Mr.
Big-ass here to sign it." They say, "Come on, lady, regulations." She says, "Voluntary my hine end." I damn near
passed out. I mean I really almost fainted. I'm hungry *all
the time.*'

His pinched face makes me sad. Those two in front
of me are still buzzing away. I am not really listening to
anything. I am wondering about chance.

I am very close to this girl, we have been whispering
confidences, soon we will be confessing to each other—
how did this happen? Was I, in the back of my mind,

19

hoping or *planning* to stand behind a girl like her when I joined the line at five in the morning? The night was overcast—dark as the bottom of the sea. I came up to the end of the line around the corner on Elm, streetlights were far away. How much could I have seen? Did I make a knowing choice? There were four columns to choose from, not so tightly packed as they are now that the street is so crowded. Might I just as well have dropped onto the next row to the left, in other words where the grandmother now stands, behind the sick-looking man who reminds me of my father? I try to think back to accidents of chance earlier this morning—for example, whatever it was in the pressure of my forefinger and thumb, turning a knob, that made me set my alarm to go off under my pillow (so as not to waken those in adjoining spaces) at four thirty-two, as it did, rather than, let's say, at four twenty-nine, in which case I would have arrived at the line three minutes earlier and missed her. I have been on the line for five mornings before this; one morning I stood behind an old lady, otherwise I have been behind men. This morning . . .

She has finished talking with the man in the bush jacket. She turns her head—to the right—and speaks just above a whisper: 'It's really interesting. He went on a company picnic the other day. They were taken in busses

20

to Madison, and while he was waiting in line to get in the men's enclosure to change into a bathing suit, this person in the line——'

'Chance,' I whisper.

'What do you mean?'

'The person he happened to be next to . . . It's a matter of chance . . .'

She puzzles a moment, pausing and cocking her head, but she apparently does not get through to the shadowy area behind what I have said. 'Anyway,' she goes on, 'this individual offered to sell our friend here a chance in a money lottery. Our friend asked to see a ticket. It was a private lottery. Our friend said, "But that's against the law." This individual said, "Not at all," and he pulled out some kind of permit, it looked airtight, had the state seal, governor's signature, it was a very good document. Our friend took a chance on it, it was clean—he was given notice of the drawing. He lost, but the point is, it was a clean operation. So our friend says he's going to put in for permission to conduct a lottery himself.'

Now I understand his seedy appearance. He is a person who makes a life of looking for loopholes. I am disappointed that the girl is so interested in his harebrained scheme.

'They'll never allow it,' I whisper.

21

'I don't know,' she says. 'How about the other individual? They let him.'

'Who's to say he didn't forge the letter?'

'With a state seal?'

'You're gullible, my dear.'

It is a weakness to soften my rebuke with an endearment.

I am thinking how hard it was for my mother to be demonstrative, but how powerful the emotion was behind her holding back. When I left home for labor duty in my sixteenth year—'home' was a single room in a boardinghouse on Howe Street; that was the last year families had rooms of their own—she said good-bye to me on the stair landing, just reached out her hand and said, 'Good-bye, son. Never forget who you are. Remember that you're a Poynter, be proud.' It was my first leave-taking, and it was to be my last. In other words, I was henceforth to be a man, I was going away once and for all. She had always kissed my cheek, or at least the air beside my cheek, each time I left the house, even just to run down to the corner on an errand for her, to get a pound and a half of ground chuck or a head of Bibb or some yogurt, in which last, by the way, she believed more fervently than she believed in her white-bearded Congregationalist God. But this time: just the handshake. Now

22

in the waitline, pressing against this girl in blue, I am hit very hard, as never before, by a realization of my mother's unshown pain in telling me that way that I was a man, and free.

THE GRANDMOTHER is trying to get the girl's attention. 'Honey,' she says. 'Say, honey!'

She aims her thick glasses at me and tells me to tell the girl she wants to speak to her. I do.

'Listen, dearie,' the grandmother says. 'It's not so easy to change jobs.'

'Did you ever notice,' I say to the grandmother, 'how everybody in the waitline for petitions is absolutely sure that everybody *else's* petition is going to be turned down?'

There is a grin on the wide barbarian face. 'They always are!'

'Then what are *you* doing here?' the girl asks with astonishing bitterness.

'Listen, I know whereof I speak. Don't think I didn't try to change jobs—just like you, dear. Not once, not twice—a dozen times. You think printing circuits was some kind of a joyride? Look at my eyes! They ruined my eyes. I'm three-quarters blind. You couldn't let through a single faulty circuit because you'd be responsible for a mass transit tie-up, or maybe something worse—you know?—it might be a speech, some high muckamuck speaking, and "due to technical difficulties there has been an interruption of the audio portion of our broadcast"? They could always trace it back. Dock you. Disgrace you. Put you back a level. . . . I tried. Oh, I tried, all right. Don't count on it, honey.'

'That's encouraging,' I sarcastically say on the girl's behalf.

The girl coldly says, 'But it's different. Mine isn't a selfish request.'

'Hah!' This comes out of Robert's grandmother's throat like a load of double-0 buckshot.

Right on top of this, the next quarter-hour siren cuts through the white sound of shuffling feet, of traffic, of caged birdsong, of voices of petitioners all up and down our waitline expressing their optimism, their hopes, their confidence in a future better than the past has been.

'That fucking sireen,' the man behind me says.

THIS GIRL gives me, who have no particular right to it yet, a pain in my chest. It is the beginning of the cre-

24

ative pain. I want to protect her, she is vulnerable. But
who knows better than I how vulnerable *I* am? I remember the voice of that girl I fell for in Niantic while I was
on labor duty—so many years ago that I forget her name.
It happened quickly, two or three evenings, an imported
Irish beer called Harp (I remember *its* name), a drive-in
movie, *The Stunner* (I remember *its* name), holding
hands at a semi-pro baseball game under lights in the
bleachered back yard of a smelly brakelining factory
(and *its* name, Bestosite), then parked somewhere and
facing each other in the unreal light from the dashboard
of the decrepit car I had wangled for the evening from
the Niantic transport pool (*its* name, Roadhawk)—the
sound of triumph in her throat: 'Yes! Yes! You have that
hurt look around your mouth!' It was not just *my* hurt
look, it was not really a hurt look at all, it was the look of
a steep fall: and she was seeing what was already, to her,
at nineteen, an old, old sign, enabling her to make yet
one more claim. . . .

This girl in the line turns her head to the right, and I
barely hear this: 'You started to tell me about your . . .
You said lawyers.'

'What can I say? I had my view of it, she had hers. I
felt she broke our contract.'

The girl nods slowly. Her head remains turned. My

25

God, I see wetness on her cheek. But surely her tears have nothing to do with me. She must have had a sudden rush of thoughts about her own mistakes with the man she couldn't hold. Or perhaps the cheerful grandmother has knocked her hopes too hard.

I cannot put my hands on her hips or waist. It is against the law. She might well turn me in.

I whisper, 'You okay?'

She nods again, then leans her head back toward me.

I feel that I must be cautious. . . . *It is strictly* . . . Does she really want me to talk about my wife? It is so hard to understand, to say nothing of trying to describe, the end of a long relationship. The girl sniffles. She seems to have controlled herself. . . . My eye is caught by the head of a monstrously tall woman in the crush of pedestrians between us and the steady stream of vehicles in the street. This woman is walking toward Elm. She has large bulbous features which blend into a surprisingly beautiful face, and she compounds her enormities with a wig which towers higher and higher into the sky. She is buffeted as she moves by the impatience and press of those around her, and her head bobs slightly as she looks now this way, now that, at the tops of the heads of the tight crowd.

26

'Look at that woman,' I say, out loud this time, to the girl. 'How calm she is!'

The woman's serenity moves me very deeply—it reaches down to the pool of strong feelings in my chest. Perhaps this serenity comes from the mere fact that her head is above all the rest of the heads, perhaps she is physically powerful and glad of it; but I think—perhaps I merely imagine—that there is something more. She has come to terms with what bothers all the rest of us. What is her secret? I wish I had the nerve to shout to her across all the people and ask her: What is your secret?

The girl, the janitor, the woman in front and to the right of me who touches both of them—this last a middle-aged schoolteacher in a brown rep dress, whose face is ravaged by a disapproving attitude she freely vents on everything—all of these, and also the man in the bush jacket, and perhaps one or two others, have heard what I said and are looking at the tall woman. In her nodding way she glances at our group and sees us staring at her. She does not smile, and the light changes in her eyes. She guards the secret.

27

I REMEMBER ONCE when I was a child my family took a trip to the sea. One morning I sat on a massive formation which the local boys called Tiger Rock. Off its end the water was deep and clear, and a network of sunlines played in constant motion on the shallower underwater boulders. There was a dark hole into which the older boys sometimes dived; I did not dare. Usually Tiger Rock swarmed with big boys, but now a hundred of them swam away with splashing and shouts, and I was alone on the rock. I held a fishing pole for a long time, with the hook and bait lowered into the hole—a bite!—and I pulled up a tiny fish, which then before my horrified eyes began to grow. It became fatter and fatter. Its dorsal fin rose erect and spiky. Its round open mouth wheezed. Its belly distended more and more. I was appalled at its anger at being lifted from its medium into mine. How could I get it off the hook and throw it back before it became as big as I? I did not call for help—the huge swarm of older boys was several yards away in the water, too noisy for my cries to reach any ears. I was paralyzed; eternity was caught on my fish hook. I remember the hugeness of the sky, my fear of the tremendous space I occupied alone and my sharper fear that this ballooning

28

fish would swell up in its anger and fill all that space, crushing me on Tiger Rock. But then the little puffer reached the limit of its protest; in truth, it was still pathetically small. The rock was suddenly teeming with boys again, and my brother disdainfully took the fish off the hook and tossed it back in the sea. It floated like a buoy for an instant, deflated itself, dived with wobbling silvery flashes into the dark abyss.

'My wife?' I whisper to the girl. 'It got so she couldn't make it with me in a room full of people. It wasn't that way at first. She changed. It was an absurd neurosis. We tried everything. I built a kind of frame and we draped sheets on it, but she could hear the people in the sleeping-hall talking and mouth-breathing in their sleep. There just wasn't any pleasure in it for her. I didn't feel I could just use her. She got desperate and began to cheat—I guess she thought that might clear things up. It's not a very nice story.'

'That doesn't tell me anything about *you*,' the girl whispers.

The janitor really stretches his neck to hear what I will whisper next.

'You mean,' I whisper, 'maybe I was the one who changed?'

'It's possible.'

29

'It's possible. You realize I have to see things from my side.'

We lived at that time in a complex on George Street. Since we had a child, our space was not bad. On one wall of the sleeping-hall were photo-murals of a rain forest in Puerto Rico—an almost palpable misty dampness, huge shiny leaves, tendrils reaching for strangleholds. My wife and I quarreled about books; both of us could read. She was an electrician on a high level of expertise: was called to work on sophisticated automated machinery. Sometimes I wondered whether having been shocked so often she had perhaps shorted out her erogenous zones.

'Are you trying to tell me that you didn't cheat?'

'Well, as the husband . . .'

'Oh, Jesus!' Vehemently whispered. What a strange name to invoke in protest against my stupid remark.

Now it is the janitor who is whispering. He inclines his head close to mine, aims his cleaver of a nose at my cheek. 'I heard you, before.'

Is he some kind of operative? Informer? I do not want to exchange whispers with this creep in a green coverall with an eagle on his shoulder, and I say out loud, 'Yes, I saw you were eavesdropping.'

But he insists on whispering. 'I mean way before. About your petition. Look, if you louse me up, I'll get you, sure as hell.'

Aloud: 'Have you fallen out of your nest?'

Whisper: 'Suppose we get to the windows exactly the same time, I'm at the window right next to you. The minute you start in, I'm done for.' He suddenly says out loud, 'We're *all* finished.'

His shoulder trembles against my shoulder. He is pale. I do not feel threatened. It is he who feels threatened. I feel depressed.

The space I occupy is near the center of the Marinson sleeping-hall. It is defined by white lines, about an inch wide, painted on the varnished pine boards of the floor. What I think of as the head of my space, because I sleep with my head in that direction, is toward the north; I sleep, in other words, parallel to Whitney Avenue. On my right, lengthwise in the hall, is the passageway, eight inches wide, to the various spaces in our row and the next one. Each person tries to give his space a private style. I have adopted a quite common practice of bunking like a seaman on top of a long chest of drawers. The distinction of my space is that, apart from this chest-bed, it is bare. It is empty. Nothing but uncovered pine boards. No desk, no chair, no rug, no lamps, no TV, no books. Nothing. I

31

have achieved a highly personal style by reducing my property—and my needs—to an absolute minimum. People think I am either pathetically poor or barren in imagination, but I have noticed that whenever I have guests, they get very high in my space, just from being in it. That is because so much of it *is* space. In a sense I have the largest home in New Haven.

But it is not large enough.

The grandmother is nudging me, and I turn toward her.

'You haven't told me what your petition is.'

The janitor's fear and anger at my petition are on my mind; I haven't dealt with him, and I don't relish at this moment the idea of setting the circuitry printer's active tongue in motion. Shall I make something up?

'I think I'd rather not discuss it.'

'You're just like my son—big Robert. He keeps things from me. Deliberately. He does it to hurt me. When little Robert was born, do you know how I found out he had come into this world? Marcia had gone to the hospital—she was having some trouble with the veins in her legs—so I called the hospital, I got the nurses' station on the floor where she was, and they said, "We aren't allowed to give out information. . . . Hold on a minute. We can put you through to your daughter-in-law when she finishes nursing." That's how I found out—they let it slip out that she had little Robert at her breast. He was already a day old. See what I mean?'

I must turn this old talkpot back on herself. 'You're so interested in everyone's petition—what's yours?'

'I'll trade. You first.' She is grinning.

I say, 'I'll bet yours is about this little Robert of yours. Right?'

'It is. Yes, it is. It's about Robert.' She pauses, then, unable to help herself, goes on. 'I don't want him to learn to read. I want him to have a useful skill.'

'I thought you were so proud he'd been chosen.'

'Of course I'm proud. But I'm also interested in his future.'

'Don't his parents have something to say?'

'They want him to read.'

'Do you always go over their heads this way?'

'I have to stay active.'

The girl has turned her head to the left and is listening. I am distracted. A deep part of my attention is drawn to the front of my body. The part of my mind that carries on with the grandmother is the stilted part devoted to manners, courtesy. I answer her only because I feel it would be rude not to. Another part, concerned with survival and courage and hope and aggression, reminds me

33

that the janitor is not at all satisfied with what I have said to him. At the edge of each layer of attention is a clamor of impressions: traffic hum, brick turrets, blue pompon, siren, sparrows, snarls from behind, resins, the nibbling of fear.

The girl says to the grandmother, 'You mean to say you're interfering this way just to keep your mind occupied?'

The glasses, like headlights, swerve and throw their baleful beams at the girl. 'What's the difference? They'll turn me down.'

The girl snorts. 'Then why stand in line this way?'

'I like it. I enter a petition lots of days. I stand on line four, five times a week. You meet people. I'm talking to you right now.'

I say, 'That's a stupid thing to do. Look at the people behind you. You may be keeping somebody away from the windows who really has a hardship case.'

She bathes me with a pitying look. 'You born yesterday? There's lots of us come all the time.'

'Can't you see that hurts everybody?'

'How hurts? Do you think you'd get a yes if I weren't here?'

This waitline, which is agony for most of us, is the

grandmother's social life. She makes me feel that my pessimism, like my attention to her words, is shallow.

I laugh and say to her, 'You're a case!'

'Listen,' she says, 'if you'd been through what I've been through . . .'

The girl is laughing, too, now.

The front I put up is earnest and hopeful, but truly I am pessimistic. Bureaucracy attracts such mediocre people; we are in the hands of imbeciles. It would make more sense to put this grandmother in charge of the petition windows than whoever is there now.

2

WE ARE STILL in the shade of the Church Street buildings; the day is going to be hot. In this weather, if one dresses for the waitline warmly enough for the early morning hours, while it is still dark and foggy, then he is bound to suffer from the heat of the forenoon. The front of my body, on which my sensory attention is focussed, is already tenderly heating up. I have no feeling at all in my back.

The breeze, when it comes, eddies capriciously, and the wisps of hair at the girl's nape are stirred now this way, now that.

The siren keens again. How much time before I must leave for work? I cannot remember. What is this girl, this urgency, doing to my inner clock?

I write reports. The job to which I must make my way is in the state building out on Bassett Street, and I write reports for my department. My desklet is in a six-by-six cubicle with walls which do not go to the ceiling—plaster divider three feet high, crinkled acrylic panels above, to a height of five feet six. The four desklets are each two feet square; one tucks one's knees under. From overhead come showers of fluorescent light and of confused sounds from all the other cubicles—a song of typewriters, calculators, duplicators, teletype machines, creaking chairs, shifting feet, clearing throats; murmurs of Acceptance with overtones of Wanting the Day to Be Done.

My reports invariably put a good face on things—their tenor goes against the grain of my pessimistic bias; perhaps that is why I occasionally have an angry stomach.

I doubt if anyone reads my reports. But if one is late I get a warning printout from the computer.

38

'I wouldn't mind changing jobs myself,' I whisper to the girl—to the right side of her face.

'I suppose everyone wants to,' she whispers. 'I suppose that's why they'll turn me down.'

'But your petition isn't a selfish one.' There is a slight note, I hope a playful one, of mockery in this echoing line.

'It *is* selfish, really,' she whispers, turning my ribbing into an accusation, 'because I don't enjoy what I'm doing now.'

She has told me that she works in a bakery. She squeezes frosting decorations onto cakes—edging, star-shaped kisses, furbelows, bunting swoops; birthday greetings, business messages, consolations. Cakes in the shapes of towers, books, sports cars, beds with covers turned down. Discussing her cakes back when we were getting acquainted, before dawn, she whispered to me, 'A lot of people have the illusion that they can make things happen by eating shapes they connect with those happenings.'

'Why would you like to change jobs?' she now asks me.

'So few higher-ups in my department can read. Who reads my reports? A good writer like me should have more readers!'

'Isn't it hard,' she whispers, veering, 'being separated from your daughter?'

'I see her on rest days'—knowing it is not enough. It
took so long—so many waitlines, less crowded ones than
this, to be sure, in those days, but slow ones all the same
—to get permission to have a child at all. Jill is twelve. I
see her in my memory as being three, or perhaps four;
her mouth is pursed as she works at weaving colored
strips of paper together. She is in the bedlam of a day-
care center, sitting cross-legged on the floor with a storm
of hundreds of children whirling around her, she is one
flake in a blizzard of innocence; yet at her weaving she is
poised, serene, concentrated. Her generation does not
seem to feel crowded. She floats in her natural medium.
Her eyes, her ears work differently from mine. She has
perceptions I cannot begin to share: Once, when she was
six, she said, 'When Jeremy claps his hands, one hand
makes more noise than the other.' In that her mind has
been shaped by a more dense and shifting time even than
mine, she and I will never understand each other. I adore
her, but I cannot alert her. And if she tries to teach me
something new, I either refuse to learn or mis-hear her;
she strikes chords in an entirely new mode, to which I am
deaf.

'What is she like?'

40

'She looks like me.' My small claim to immortality.

'But that doesn't tell me anything. I can't see your face.'

Of course that is true. Since well before dawn we have been so close-packed that the girl has not been able to turn her head far enough around to get a good look at me. I find this disturbing. The pressure of my body against hers does not tell her what sort of person I am; her sense of me comes only from what she hears in my voice. It is true that I don't know how wide her face is, but at least I can *see*: the wisps of fine hair at her neck, the sky on her skin, the bump that I presume to be related to humor on the left side of her face. The three-quarters rear view shows her to be an easy person—no tense muscles, no started veins. The sight of her flesh so close to my own—her cheek, the side of her neck—makes her real and helps me define her.

She has seemed responsive. I remember how, a while ago, she leaned her head back toward me, when I put out a few sympathetic syllables at her sudden puzzling grief. But how can she come to have any feelings about me—negotiable feelings, I mean—without seeing me and perhaps being encouraged by what she sees?

'What do you imagine I look like?'

'Mmmm. You're six feet two.'

41

'You can *feel* that. What about my face?'

'Dark brown hair?'

'How did you know?'

'I didn't. I shot from the hip. There aren't so many possibilities, you know. Black. Dark brown. Light brown. Blond. Three-to-one shot.'

'Or gray.'

'You don't sound gray.'

'Or red.'

'Definitely not. I mean, I *know* you're not a redhead. . . . Let's not play this game. I'd rather imagine your face. You're like a character in a novel: I have to create your face for myself.'

'But then when you see me . . .'

'You'll be in the movie made from the book.'

'You won't like seeing a different face from the one you've made up.'

'If it's a good movie it won't matter.'

I have a flash of line-fear. . . . It was not exactly fear that time; it was some kind of transmuted rage. Yet it was terror, too. Anger is frightening because we citizens have been lectured so often about the equivalence of control and survival. The slogan word, Acceptance, is a code word for steel—for that hard alloy of obedience and courage without which we could not live in circum-

42

stances like ours. This line-fear can build on itself; a person in a waitline can arrive at a pitch of frustration and desperation so towering as to tilt him over into a sensation of being frozen for eternity in a *condition* of waiting —and, what is most terrifying, a condition of waiting for something not worth waiting for. We have come to speak of this sensation as waitline sickness. One who is stricken in a line by this affliction can only stand there and scream. I have not been driven nearly so far as that, but I was frightened, for a fleeting moment there, of being trapped forever in this waitline, because of my rage at the grotesque imbalance in my relationship with the girl, which the line imposes on us. The line denies her one sense of me—the central sense.

A ND SO I WONDER what the man behind *me* looks like. I cannot see him. I have a cartoon of him in my mind, sketched on the basis of the bitter short commands he barks out from time to time. Turning my head as far as I can, and my eyes in my head as much farther as they will swing, I bring his head into the edge of my field of vision. I try with great concentration to sharpen my peripheral perception, and I do make out a pale ellipse, and

43

yes, I see that there *is* a nose, there *are* dark pools where eyes should be, but I cannot bring the features into focus. Is the hair gray? My heart sinks. That sort of blur is all I can be to her. I am frustrated by my failure to incarnate that narrow oval behind me, and I am angry that my own face cannot come to life in the girl's eyes. I am sorry for myself, I am even a bit sorry for the blur behind me—and this weak push of compassion for someone who, like myself, cannot be seen for what he is, rouses in me a curiosity about him which I have, up to now, denied myself.

Over my shoulder I speak to him. 'Hey, what's eating you? Why are you in such a hurry?'

Then I realize that without thinking, I have turned my head to the right to ask these questions, and the janitor believes I am asking them of him. Already convinced that my petition will queer his, he is obviously taken aback by the challenge in my questions.

'It's easy enough for you,' he shouts in my face, with his two eyes wedged between my two. 'You're in the second row. You ought to try being on the outside. I got all these people moving the wrong way. You get jostled out here. My whole right arm is futzed up.'

I shake my head no, as if I were trying to plug one of my eyes after another into the narrow two-holed electrical outlet the janitor's eyes make. 'No,' I say, 'I'm talking to the man behind me. Hey, I'm talking to you behind me there!'

Nothing.

I repeat.

Then from him a sharp 'What?'

'Why are you in such a hurry? Ever read about the whiting and the snail?'

'Huh?'

'Can you read? Did you ever read—?'

'I'm a painter! Color!'

I want to see him in my mind. 'How old are you?'

No answer. I don't know whether I will hear any-thing more—aside from his bursts of impatience—from the painter. The janitor is still trying to burn me with looks.

But I keep my head turned right, and now I realize why the girl has been turning that way so much of the time to speak to me. This way is *outward*. Buildings loom to the left. There is much distracting motion to the right, but the bigger sky is there—fleecy clouds now, slowly drifting northeastward; the pleasingly tapered wooden steeples; the wide idea of the lawn beyond the wall.

'Thirty-six.'

He has answered after all. He is one year younger than I. He is at the age when husbands split up with their wives.

'Do you paint houses or pictures?'

A short pause, then: 'Anything wrong with both?'

'You paint both? How do you have time?'

'Keep moving! Let's keep this line moving!'

So *that* is his itch—trying to cram two lives into one lifetime.

After a few moments I say to him, 'Can you give me a word picture of yourself?'

'What's biting you?' he bursts out. 'All these questions all of a sudden.'

'We've been here how long—four hours and some? I don't know, I just want to have a mental picture of somebody I've been up against all morning. I mean an accurate one.'

'Look. I charge money for portraits.'

His voice is edgy. I will have to settle for imagining his looks, as the girl chooses to imagine mine. Yes, I think I see him. There is something wrong with his mouth. But what do *I* look like? I feel as if my face is gradually dissolving.

46

SHE IS TALKING to the teacher on her right. The question that opens the way to acquaintance in the wait-line has been exchanged between these two. I gather that the teacher's petition has to do with conditions in her classroom. The policeman who has been assigned to her room has never before had school duty; he has come straight off the streets in a precinct where self-discipline is wanting. 'He shouts for silence,' this disapproving woman says. 'You can't *shout* for quiet. Shouting begets shouting. My room has gotten to be like a stadium.'

I am impressed by the intensity of her hatred of the policeman. I fear for some of her pupils.

The girl says, 'I could never concentrate in school. I used to look out the window all the time. I have a kind of album in my head of all the views from all the school windows I spent all those years staring out of.'

'This line is all wrong,' the teacher says. 'They ought to make it eight across. Detour the pedestrians around through Orange Street. Move us through faster.'

At her absurd logic I jump out of the confinement of my four touchers and say, 'That wouldn't move us any faster. People would take just as long at the petition windows as they do now.'

The teacher swivels her head back toward me, and I believe I might prefer imagining her full face to seeing it. 'I was talking to this young lady.'

'I couldn't help overhearing you. Forgive me, but to move us faster it would be necessary to increase the number of windows.'

The teacher gives me such a teacherish look that I feel obliged to volunteer a bad-boy addition to what I have already said. 'Besides, Orange Street is filled to capacity every morning as it is. You couldn't force another body in it with a crowbar.'

My impertinence gives the girl the beginnings of giggles of the involuntary sort children sometimes get in serious settings—at concerts, lectures, funerals. The teacher looks at her, at me, back at her. The girl laughs as apologetically as she can.

Perhaps I should feel clever. Instead I decide I may be growing quarrelsome. I am conscious of the janitor still bristling on my right. I try to mollify the teacher. 'I agree that the line is terribly slow.'

'All waitlines are slow,' she says, as if saying, 'You believe the earth is flat.'

The girl is bringing her laughter under control. She ends it with some sniffles much like those at the end of

48

her weeping a short while ago. Is she subject to hysteria
—the most serious failing of all in a crowd?

No one needs to be told that waitlines are slow. We
are allowed fifteen minutes at table for breakfast at the
Marinson; it takes twenty-five minutes in the cafeteria
line to get to the first food racks. We are allowed six minutes on the john; there is a twenty-minute wait in the
shitline. There should be more petition windows, no
doubt of that. There should be more of everything. But
there is not more of everything. That is the first fact of existence.

' MY WIFE,' I whisper, 'was too damned judicious.'

I remember, once, on a rest day, a sunny morning in
May, when the dogwood was at its height—we sat over
breakfast and discussed a choice: Should we take Jill to
Judges' Cave State Park, or should we stay in town and
take a chance on a waitline at the public library? Doris
considered. She didn't *list* all the pros and cons out loud.
It was more a case of, 'Let's see . . . ,' 'Let me think
about it a sec . . . ,' 'Mmmm . . .' An atmosphere of
good sense, not rushing blindly into things. Many long
silences. Many incomplete utterances—blurted frag-

49

ments to convey some kind of mulling under the surface. Time passed. Very good. It was now too late to get on the line for the busses to Judges' Cave. Relief all around; we were reduced to the single issue: library or no? Now there was some less sketchy discussion. We have taught Jill to read ourselves—have we pushed her too fast? Should we ease up awhile? There are few books suitable for ten-year-olds; mostly they bore Jill. Maybe she is getting pale from living in shadows; maybe she should see a bit more raw life. Our past experience with the library waitline has been discouraging. . . . Many considerations. We asked Jill to help us settle it. She sighed. Looked at the ceiling. Balanced views were further refined—until we looked at the clock and saw that it was now too late to get on the library line. Immense relief—a second decision made by default. We finally went for a walk and were all cranky—raw life.

'Whatever there was to say on any subject, you could count on her response: "There's another point of view, Sam."' I want to go on to say, You can guess what it was like when there was some really important issue to settle: Shall we ask for permission to have a baby? Weeks, months, literally years—we had the baby too late, our relationship was already . . . But I whisper no more about this problem which has caused me so much pain.

50

The girl does not answer. It seems to me that she is laughing!

I am embarrassed, and I blunder on. 'That's my side of it, anyway. I bet you're going to say, "Maybe there's another point of view, Sam." Maybe you think I had a lot to do with her vacillation. . . .'

She really is laughing.

'Going through all that has made me impulsive,' I whisper. My impulse at this moment is to make a move of some kind in this girl's direction. The warmth at the front of my body has begun to be focussed. I have a strong urge to break the law. The girl is laughing silently. I do not get any strong encouragement from this silent laughter. Would she report me?

This possibility shocks me. I must get a grip on myself. I think of the janitor's hostility—that will serve. I turn my eyes on him, and that is enough. He explodes.

But just before he does, she says out loud, 'I didn't know your name was *Sam!*' She is laughing hard.

His outburst is all the more violent in that it is hissed in whispers.

'Get out of the line.'

This does the trick. My desire modulates swiftly into a reaction of anger mixed with alarm. My tumid flesh shrinks; I push out my chin.

The girl has heard and has stopped laughing without sniffles.

'Are you crazy? After waiting since five in the morning?'

The janitor sprays me with spit as he tries to keep his next whisper even more hushed. 'You *can't* ask for more space. You'll have us all in trouble. They'll shut the petition windows. Or something much worse. I'm telling you, you better get out of this line before I get you out.'

I try to be cool. 'Anyone has a right to be in the line.'

'Not to ask *that*. You have no right to spoil everyone else's chances.'

'How would I be spoiling your chances? You're asking for food.'

A torrent is loosed. He forgets to whisper. 'You damn fool, *you know why*. Who cares about food? What kind of space do you think *I* have? When I had to put my wife away, the very day, I mean, Christ, two hours after I got back from Connecticut Valley, they cut me down to a single person's space. I tell you I wasn't home two hours—I was *famished*, just lying down trying to get my strength back—and here comes this twerp in a gray uniform from Allocations. He had two porters with him, and they carted my wife's stuff and my stuff away right then —I had no comeback, he had a warrant all made out—to this single space that they'd just moved some other guy out of, three houses down Willow Street. Look, in the married-couple space we'd had, we were so tight you had to climb over things—you had to move the TV and the vacuum cleaner onto the bed if you wanted to use the table, and the other way around, you know, back and forth. God, we worked hard for things, a lot of years, it's not so easy to give things up when they've come hard. So we had all our stuff piled up as it was. Well, when they put all our junk in a *single* space, it had to be really stacked. I can't get *at* anything now. It isn't any more, you know, moving things back and forth—it's stacking and unstacking. The rocking chair has to be on top of the pile, it isn't steady enough to pile anything on—it *rocks*. You know? I can't get rid of anything. I hope she'll get better. I miss her. I want her back. Let her throw stuff at me. If she comes back we'll get space for two again—but not in any two hours, I'll tell you *that*. I've seen people get married and have to make do with single space for *six months* waiting for what's their everyday right.'

The janitor is almost shouting. His face is close to mine, his great machete of a nose is swinging dangerously, his cheeks are hectic, his upper lip works like the foot of a sewing machine.

O̲v̲e̲r̲ ̲h̲e̲r̲ ̲s̲h̲o̲u̲l̲d̲e̲r̲ the teacher says to the janitor, 'Shut up!'

'Stop your bellyaching!' the painter behind me, who has been doing nothing but bellyaching all morning, snaps. There has been a difference, of course: The painter has merely been impatient about the slowness of the line; the janitor has been touching on an unbearable subject.

Others near us grumble.

The janitor's face is bleak. I can imagine that he is suffering sudden hunger pangs in the face of the hostility that he has, in the thoughtless single-mindedness of his tirade against me, drawn on himself. There is a rapt quality in his bleakness. He has perhaps a vision of a delicacy that will assuage his appetite—terrapin stew and corn bread come into my mind. Strange choice; once in my life have I eaten terrapin stew. Am I so hungry myself? Of course I am glad to have the janitor's threats to me cut off, at least for the moment.

54

THE IMMEDIATE use I make of his threats is to remind myself that I must be more than ever careful with
the girl, who is less apt to turn me in, after all, than the
janitor now is if he detects the slightest sign of impropri-
ety on my part.

I am a signaler in search of a code.

I murmur close to her left ear, 'When I was ten I
wanted more than anything on earth to have the power
of flight. May I tell you a story? A girl named Deborah
lived in the room next to ours, she was older than I, she
must have been fourteen or fifteen. She visited us one afternoon, my mother was at home, and Deborah talked
mostly with her. For a while Deborah lay down on the
daybed I slept on at night. That night when I went to bed
I did two things at once. One was that I lay on my stomach and prayed to God—I believed in Him only when it
came to needing things—to please, please let me fly, and
during my prayer I saw myself, arms outspread, soaring
around the Knights of Columbus Tower and then higher,
just above the shoulder of East Rock—I was in an ecstasy;
the air was somehow thick, amber-colored, I sailed in a
kind of twilight; I can't describe to you the joy I felt.
. . . Then the other thing was that while I was praying

55

and seeing myself above everything I was also kissing every square inch of the part of the bed where Deborah had put down her head for two minutes.'

'God didn't do you much good, did He?'

'No, He didn't. I got mad at Him.'

'I never wanted anything like that,' she murmurs. 'I'm more of a realist.'

Realist. I say to myself, That word does not describe a decipherer, does it? Could it be that this girl is not too bright? It takes a surprisingly long time to detect stupidity of certain sorts in a person. Drawing back, I murmur, 'Deborah turned out to be quite ugly. I saw her a couple of days ago. She's fat and disappointed-looking.'

'I wanted to be a movie star. Did you ever see any of those old Marilyn Monroe pictures?'

'That's realistic?'

She laughs. 'Even realists dream sometimes.'

Yes, I did once see several Monroe movies that were shown by a street film society I belonged to. Our society specialized in old pictures from that era, showing so much air space enveloping people, so much sheer chilling distance between characters. I remember the pictures well. *Knock on Any Door. Niagara. Bus Stop. The Misfits.* One saw Marilyn Monroe ripen from film to film, till finally the fruit in the bottle of air was bruised. Vision

56

is the primary sense. Watching those films, I always wanted less distance between myself and Marilyn Monroe's breasts. I am an American man-baby. I have no image yet of this girl's breasts. She is a realist; in mentioning Marilyn Monroe she must have had something in mind. I incline my head to the left and over her shoulder, but without being offensive I cannot crane far enough, and anyway her breasts are hidden in the pleats of the bush jacket. *It is strictly forbidden* to reach one's hands forward and around. . . .

'Yes, I saw her a few times—film society we used to have. I've seen her on the tube, too, years ago.' But I am distracted by those pleats in the lottery man's jacket. 'I won a TV set in a lottery once,' I whisper. 'I took two tickets, a buck apiece.'

'You're just naturally lucky,' she whispers.

'Yes,' I whisper. 'I just am.'

Imagination is more important than reason; I do not really care if she is a bit dumb, as long as she is imaginative. We'll see. Right now I am imagining something which requires no intelligence at all, something which is not permitted, even in imagination, to either man or woman *while in accidental or formal etcetera.* . . . But dimensions have been added to my daydream; I now feel more than mere lust. . . . What else? An explicit curios-

57

ity; sympathy; free-floating emotions—the diffusion of that generous pain in my chest.

The grandmother's glasses are turning my way. With such powers of magnification before her eyes, can she see this obsession growing in me? And I ask myself, Does it matter that it is this particular girl? Were I to be pressed up against *any* girl in a waitline, any moderately healthy young woman of an age not greater than mine, not much greater, anyway, would I be making the same explorations of her whole being, building helplessly toward the same obsessive focusing of my desire? I am appalled by something random in my nature that comes out in a crowd.

ONCE WHEN I worked for the travel agency,' the grandmother says, 'a man came in who said he wanted a ticket to Katmandu. I'd never even heard of such a place. He was an ornithologist. There was one kind of bird he'd been chasing for thirty years.'

This old party is not too pleased with her position in the waitline. Her touchers lack sociability. The decrepit gent in the black suit in front of her is like my father in more than appearance: He is a hopeless conversationalist. He agrees with everything she says to him. I have seen him nodding to get rid of her nattering. I do not want to concern myself with the grandmother's other two touchers, but it is evident that they also are too tight-lipped for her taste. She seems to have a rather desperate hope that she can stir up a storm of talk in me. The price of my having tried to see the girl's breasts over her left shoulder is going to be listening to this story of the ornithologist who wanted to go to Nepal.

The point of the story, alas, seems only to be that those were the good old days when you never had to wait more than a month for a reservation to fly anywhere in the world.

'What bird was he hoping to find?'

'He told me, but I don't remember.'

I do not think she has seen into my heart, or trousers. She is not interested in the ornithologist's splendid obsession, to say nothing of my workaday one.

Having come to this conclusion, I am startled when suddenly she says, 'You two get along pretty good, don't you?'

At this the girl's head quickly turns left.

I could not tell from the grandmother's tone of voice how loaded her comment was. 'What makes you think that?' I ask her in a guarded voice.

'All that whispering.'

It seems best to tell the truth. 'That's just to have a conversation with one person. You and I are different. You like to talk to everybody. I like to talk to one person. That's the only reason I've been whispering to this young lady.'

'Why don't you whisper to me?' The huge eyes smile; behind the magnifying lenses I see the indistinct trembling of a quinquegenarian flirtatiousness. *She* can see what the girl cannot—my face. Is she attracted to it, and to me? This idea is awful. Once when I was fifteen and thought that I enfolded in my young package of flesh the entire range of human sexual and emotional energy, I worked a summer vacation as a delivery boy for the branch of Sears in Hamden—this was when families still had separate rooms—and one day I delivered an electric batter mixer to a rooming house on Edgehill Terrace, where a woman who must have been twenty years older than I was at home alone. It was hot and she had on just a light caftan zipped down the front, and holding me in conversation she suddenly opened the front of it and showed me her body. She came close to me. Excited, I fled. I was horrified by the idea that a woman that old would have rampant sexual desires—and capacities. If she was more or less twenty years my senior, she may

60

have been, on that day, let's say, thirty-seven. I am thirty-seven now. When I am fifty-seven, how long will the waitlines be? And what if I stand on one of them then, even more tightly packed than now, beside, or behind, an attractive woman of thirty-seven, or a beautiful girl of seventeen?

I feel a bit low in spirits, but I force myself to joke with Robert's grandmother. 'I wouldn't dare,' I whisper to her. 'You'd tell all.'

THE GIRL has heard this, as I intended, and she laughs.

The grandmother, however, does not laugh. She turns away. It seems I have hurt her feelings by my blunt statement that I wish to speak to only one person, and she is not that person. But she has a rubber core, she is soon bouncing into a new relationship off to her left, with a toucher of one of her touchers.

The girl asks me in a very quiet murmur over her left shoulder, 'How do you plan to justify your petition?'

'I don't know yet.'

'You mean you don't go up to the petition windows with what you're going to say all memorized?'

61

'I've never been to the windows before.'

'You've never entered a petition?'

'Not for years—not since it was all in writing. I've been on this line the last five mornings, but I didn't make it to the windows.'

'You'll make it this morning. This is really your first time?'

'Yes, really.'

'You must have led a charmed life! . . . I don't like it. They call them windows, but you can't see whatever it is on the other side. They have these bars and then glass. I suppose it's the one-way-vision kind of glass that they use to watch experiments through—you know?—psychological experiments? The whoever with the voice can see you, but you can't see him—or her. And yet the voice comes through as if there were nothing but air between you and him, or her. Weird! I remember, last time, I could overhear the conversations at the windows on either side—the windows are close together—and the voices from beyond the bars and the glass there sounded exactly like the one that was speaking to me. Thin, like a lawyer talking, in between man and woman. But it's not mechanical. I don't see how it could be. The questions are so rapid-fire, so searching, and they're so responsive to whatever you say. The terrible thing is the speed with which

the voice finds its way to the weakness of your argument.
I can't even remember now what the weakness of mine
was, last time—you know, about moving closer to my job;
in fact, I'm not sure it *was* weak. But the voice convinces
you it is; it breaks down your belief in your own desires.
And then it says, in the most offhand and unfeeling way,
'Petition denied. Next!' And you turn away, you feel like
you're going to choke—you feel as if you'd known all
along that that would be the outcome, that what you'd
asked for was bad for New Haven, bad for everyone, had
been from the very start.'

'Do you have that feeling this morning—ahead of
time, I mean? About your petition to change jobs since
you can't move?'

'The old spoilsport next to you doesn't seem to think
I have much chance, does she?'

How can I claim more space than my neighbors? Already convinced that I have the largest home in New Haven, how can I want an even larger one? Well . . . I am
special. I have valuable gifts. I am a writer. I need scope.
I need room to think.

What will the thin, epicene, lawyerish voice say to
those assertions? Will there be laughter behind the
glass?

63

It was my mother who gave me the conviction that I am special. She did this not so much with words as by an endless series of hand signals—a tap of praise on the arm at the right moment; dirt cleaned off my chin by a licked finger; a magician's palm waved mysteriously over my head, as if she might at any moment pull a live rabbit out of it. She had confidence-giving fingertips. She believed in work, trust, printed words, forgiveness, and, as I have said, yogurt. Except for a bit of hypochondria, brought on, I believe, by her tendency to blame herself for my father's errors, a weakness which he forgave her, she seemed not to have any serious worries. I was one of the lucky sons.

My father, who did worry, paradoxically gave me courage. He had good reason to be fearful and to pretend not to be—Parkinson's disease. In his tremorous suffering and uncertainty he sent me messages I have never forgotten—and now, knowing that defending my dangerous petition will take some of the staunchness he transmitted, I am so grateful to him that I am willing to move again outside of the box of my four touchers and make

some contact with the man in front of the circuitry printer, who has reminded me of him.

I approach him through the girl with a whisper.
'What's the fellow on your left petitioning for?'

'Cigars.'

I cannot whisper a laugh; I make it heard. Then I
murmur, 'That's one petition that ought to get by.'

'I doubt it. He wants *imported* cigars. Havanas.'

'Come on.'

'Ask him then.'

'Tell him I want to know why Havanas.'

She speaks to him, and his head slowly turns.

I see him fresh, and I am astonished at how inaccurate my first impression was. His face is wider and round-
er than my father's. His eyes make an appeal, then the
whole face breaks into a grin—the question about the Havanas has brought out a corner-cutter's canny vigor. I
would bet that he likes practical jokes. Makes friends
easily. Covertly evades regulations. A fullness under the
jaw, a hearty fold of flesh of a man who eats the fat along
the edge of the steak, is tightened by the grin, and the
face is immensely attractive. There is corruption in it,
and cruelty, but not sickness.

'You smoke?' he asks me.

65

'You think I'm crazy?'

He squints. 'I have no way of judging.' Then he adds, 'Yet.' And gives a laugh that is like a hungry man's bite.

'Why Havanas?'

'My mouth—I'm going to have to turn it in for a pants pocket.' The appeal, the cruel relish, linger in and about the eyes. 'Tampas, Puerto Ricanos, those terrible firecrackers they're putting out in Georgia now—all the so-called native specials. They just make your mouth into an incinerator. Look.'

Suddenly he hangs out a dog's length of singed flannel tongue.

'You need Havanas,' I say. 'I can see that.'

'What I like about Havanas,' he says, through a grin, 'they're so hard to get.'

He is not the least bit like my father. He is coarse and selfish. I dislike his likableness, I am actually quite angry with him for being unlike my father.

There is something besides that Cape Cod sand dune at the edge of my mind about my father and space. How big our room on Howe Street was by today's standards! Within those four walls I watched the stealth of his sickness. He and it were always there when I got home from school. His disease was a powerful wrestler. I

66

stayed as much as possible on the other side of the room from their grappling. My father kept looking up from the match, telling me to study, use a better light to read by, practice my violin. One day he told me in a shaky voice, 'It's not hereditary, Sam.' Having indeed been fearful that the wrestler might at some moment let go his terrible half-nelson on my father and suddenly raise me up, whirl me in the air, and throw me to the ground in the manner of a bearded wrestler with his sodden victim I once had seen on television, I considered this good news, and after that I let myself move a bit closer to him. He sat at our eating table and wrote poetry in a longhand which, because of his tremor, no one could read, not even he. I did my homework on the opposite side of the table. Sometimes he kissed me goodnight. The pulsations of the tremor in his neck muscle worked his bristles on my cheek like sandpaper.

I wonder: Why did I think the man in front of the grandmother was so like my father? Could it be that he is like the man my father was but is unlike my memory of what he was?

Now i think i see the thrust of the first question everyone asks in this waitline. Acquaintance is not the aim. To know another's petition is to push him away from oneself. Here is knowledge that creates space. There is not only a girl, there is also a thick pillar of antipathy, between me and the man who wants to set up a money lottery; I am very far indeed from a desire to keep Robert's nose out of books; there is an ocean, or perhaps a generation, between me and the Havana man.

I am far from all of them, but are they far from me? They all want what I want.

Between me and the girl there are only a couple of layers of cloth. Her petition does not distance me as much as some of these others' do, as the petition for protein on my right does, for example. I am well enough fed; hungry sometimes but never weak. But like the girl I would gladly change jobs, knowing however that I would then soon gladly change jobs all over again. Her petition does not make her distant, it only makes her seem short-sighted. I am sure that she, like me, would wish to have more space. I am happy that our two petitions do not so much separate us. I do not want more space between us. I want to be close to her; to enter her.

3

Up to the left, the tall black man in the red cap with a blue pompon is tipping out big dollops of excitement to those around him. His head snaps back and forth; when it turns our way, we see his active tongue and teeth more clearly than his eyes.

Some message ripples back along the line from him. One can see the faces flashing, the mouths working, but there is no meaning yet in this agitation which moves like a puff of wind along the surface of our stream of people.

Now the crest of the urgency is coming closer.

Around comes the face of the Havana-cigar man. He looks at me as he says, 'Woman's fainted. Wedged in. Pass the word back to ease up so they can get her out.'

I turn my head and speak for the first time to a toucher of touchers of mine to my left rear, behind the grandmother and next to the painter. This is a good-looking young man of about twenty, I would say, with a large dark mustache that droops down on either side of his mouth. I give him the message, and his head turns to relay it.

As this young man's eyes swing away from mine, I am struck by the thought that most of the people in the waitline for the petition windows are middle-aged. He and the girl are fairly young; all the others around me are getting on; and so am I.

Fainting in waitlines is one hazard of our lives that brings out an automatic compassion in everyone. I try, as I assume everyone else is now trying, to push backward. My feet give me little leverage. The forward pressure of the line all morning has been expressive of hope, of melioristic optimism, of thoughts of a bearable future, and now the effort to push back seems to me to be bearish, foreboding. I do not want to pull away from the girl. I say to her out loud, 'We ought to try to push back.'

70

'I'm trying,' she says. 'You're in the way.'

I laugh at her joke, and I am pleased at her aware-ness of me as a force of resistance.

Gradually, minutely, as the wave of the appeal moves back along the line, the pressure eases, but we re-apply it, backward now, to give as much relief as possible up ahead where the woman has fainted.

The man in the cap is struggling, the pompon wag-gles. Little by little we see in front of him a body lifted straight upward, like a cork from a bottle's neck—a loll-ing head with hair disarranged, an ashen face, shoulders in white, a slender waist. Arms reach up on all sides to prop the limp form. For a time there is an impasse; the unconscious woman floats upright, hip-high, in the air.

Then her body, held up by stanchions of many arms, is eased out flat and is passed to the right over the heads of those in the line.

But this is no help. The two pedestrian streams, one moving toward Elm Street and one toward Chapel, are as tightly packed as our waitline. Traffic is solid in the street and moving at the regulated rate. There is no room anywhere to let the body down. It is carried slowly over-head, like an honored corpse in a Wagner opera, for a time in one direction, then for a time in the other.

Out of the press and up in the air the woman revives.

71

She happens to be quite near us, lying up there on up-raised hands, when she comes to, and I see on her face a blurred look of amazement. She must wonder if she inhabits a dream. The last she remembers from before she fainted must be of standing tight-pressed in the line; doubtless she had been talking petitions, knew her touchers and some of their touchers, was encouraged by the closeness to the bureau building. Now, after a brief voyage in darkness, she wakes up high in the air, on a couch of tense palms, moving toward Elm Street and the end of the line.

People are shouting all sorts of contradictory advice. I hear the painter behind me shout, 'To the windows! Heist her to the windows!'

This, from the crotchety complainer, is surprisingly generous, yet also practical. At the petition windows, and only there in this whole block, can she be let down to stand on the ground.

I am confused. I want to help pass the painter's message to those pedestrians near us who are now holding up the woman, but there is so much shouting that it seems futile for me to raise my voice.

The janitor turns his head around toward the painter, at his left rear, and says, 'You got a good idea there.

The only way—we got to shout in unison. Like a ball game, right? Kill the ump, right?' His eyes sparkle; he is greatly enjoying himself. 'Everybody shout!' he shouts. 'To the windows! To the windows! To the windows!' With difficulty he raises his arms and begins beating time like a cheerleader, or indeed like a baseball fan leading a chant for the murder of a wall-eyed umpire; he also marks the bursts by nodding his head in rapid jerks. I smell his armpit close beside my face.

I catch his exuberance and join in, and the painter does, and the girl does, and the grandmother does—and so, after a few pulses of the cry, do others in the line, as they understand the point of what we are urging. Our chant becomes jaunty and irresistible.

But it is only we in the waitline who have our minds so tightly bound to the windows. Most of the pedestrians have no idea what we mean by 'windows.' Some seem to think we mean the windows looking into the Green across the street; I see some bearers' heads turn that way. Perhaps they think that we think that the sight of the empty expanse of lawn would restore one who had succumbed to crowd pressure. But it is absurd! How get her there through the traffic?

The woman herself immediately understands

the shouts, and a look of cunning and eagerness erupts on her still pallid face. She writhes, trying to give instructions to those who are supporting her.

The pedestrians whose hands now hold her are hoping to get to various destinations, and they are baffled by the chant now being roared by hundreds of petitioners. As if by common consent, they resolve their uncertainty by discarding the woman and the problem; if the people in the line are so vocal, let them handle her and it. The bearers unceremoniously roll her back onto the waitline, a little behind where we are.

At once the petitioners, laughing now, begin propelling her forward. She is being bounced and rolled. It is a game. She squeals with pleasure that sounds like alarm, like someone being tossed in a blanket. She knows that her swoon is paying off. She will reach the windows much sooner than she would have otherwise.

She goes over us, and I get my hands on her. Her thighs are soft, a bit clammy. This shaking up will restore her circulation.

She moves quickly up the line. The excitement in our vicinity gradually subsides.

Still cheered by our spirit of cooperation, I congratulate the janitor for his presence of mind in organizing the chant. 'I'm really impressed,' I say.

74

'You son of a bitch,' he says. 'Are *you* still in the line? We ought to lift you out and send you the hell back that way.' He slants his head back toward Elm Street.

Cooperation? With a mental shiver I remember his gleeful phrase, the icy light in his eyes, 'Kill the ump!'

Now there is some kind of ruckus at the doors of the bureau building, where I can see the woman still supported overhead. Can it be that the people at the front of the line, having waited more than four hours for their chances at the windows, refuse to let her into a position ahead of theirs?

At last she is passed in, still overhead, through one of the doors. She does not re-emerge, she must have been given room. . . . I wonder what she is asking for, standing in front of the bars and the one-way glass.

Now THAT I have seen how knowing others' petitions gives a little distance from them, I am able to have some curiosity about another toucher of touchers of mine —the young man with the handlebar mustaches to whom I passed the word on the woman's having fainted a few minutes ago.

I turn and ask him the required question.

'My wife and I—putting in for a baby,' he says.

'This the first time you've asked?'

'Yeah.'

'I've been through that meat grinder. I have a child. It's rough. When my wife and I were asking for permission it was done in a different way—they had a special bureau. It was all paperwork then. Fill out a form. Rejected—answers incomplete. Try again. Rejected—insufficient tax stamps. Try again. Rejected—one signature illegible. They never said we couldn't have a baby, just kept finding technicalities.'

'I know,' the young man says. 'Everyone tells me it won't happen the first time. May never. It must be a lot tighter now than when you tried.'

He sees me as an aging man. My pessimism asserts itself. 'It took us three years,' I say, 'even back then.'

'We don't care. We want to try.'

'What makes you want to bring a baby into . . . ?' My chin points in three wide swoops at the stream of people waiting.

'We think trying'll make our sex more—you know—three-dimensional.'

'How's that again?'

'*You* know—function of the testes, manufacture sperm. Her cycle, the ovum comes down to look for

76

sperm. It's *nature*. We think we can have a lot better or-
gasms if—well, *you* know.'

Now I have my distance from the young man, and I
breathe easier.

'It's already better,' he says. 'I mean, just talking
about the petition, the *idea*—it already has trickled down
from our heads into our—you know. I mean, last night,
instead of foreplay we discussed the petition, and then
we started in and she came like a thunderclap, it almost
knocked her into the next space where this old carpenter
lives. I mean it almost killed her the way she came. See
what I mean? It wasn't all that good for me, I mean I
came, it was maybe a six-throbber, no world-beater, but
she was really sweet to me after, and the whole thing was
good. We think it'll really make a difference.'

'Good luck,' I say, 'raising the kid.'

I turn back to the girl. 'Did you hear that?' I murmur to her.

'No, what?'

'I was talking with this lunk back here . . .' And I
begin to tell the girl what the young man with the handlebar mustaches has said. But I find as I get into the sto-

77

ry that I am suddenly shy, I cannot force the thunderclap and the six throbs out through my larynx. The account loses its point.

Some strange flotsam, however, apparently gets through the net of my reticence, because when I have finished, the girl says, 'I sucked my thumb until I was nearly ten. Put me to sleep. Do you love sleep as much as I do?'

'I'm a light sleeper,' I tell her.

We confide to each other quirks of our night life in our separate beds; my heart begins to beat rapidly. She is courageous, more open than I, and she begins to tell me about her capers with men. She has frankly not had much luck. For openers, there was a hairy slob, a kind of sex pickpocket. She is not going to get the advantage of me by boasting, that is immediately certain. Her first big love was an oaf who didn't know how emotion lubricates the way to the egg; through ignorance he was a cruel rapist. She taught him, and his gratitude turned him against her. Next . . .

Her recital of miseries has an undercurrent of primeval rage, but I do not feel threatened by it, any more than I was by the janitor's more practical hostility. Quite the opposite; I respond to her in a new way altogether. It occurs to me that I could be an exception. I am willing to

78

believe it. The layers of cloth between us are becoming thinner.

She has an onanistic habit, about which she gives me only oblique hints. It is some kind of ritual of self-indulgence; a mirror is involved; something about a childhood heroine of hers on whom she had what she calls 'a crush'; bust measurements, her heroine's then, her own now—I cannot make it all out, but I am touched by her unsuccessful effort to confess. Without even having seen my face, she is trying hard to give me a gift of trust.

LOUDLY THE TEACHER asks, 'What time is it?'

It is obvious that the teacher does not like my whispering in the girl's right ear. She has doubtless heard a bit too much of what the girl has just whispered back to me. I must assume that she is still put out with me for having set her straight on her plan to speed up the wait-line.

'The last siren must have been . . . Let's see . . .' I am glad to discover that the girl, like me, has lost track of time; she turns and asks the cigar man.

'Getting on for a quarter to,' he says. He is not one to lose track. He is a speculator; he licks his lips and blinks.

79

I am sure he has made a bet with himself about the girl. I can almost feel, vectored to me, the lewd pressure of his arm against hers.

She tells the teacher what he has said.

'Really?' the teacher says. 'Can it be?' It seems to be in her nature to find whatever is said mistaken.

'You sure of the time?' the girl asks the cigar man.

'Sure I'm sure,' he says.

'I would have thought,' the teacher says to him across the girl, 'that it was almost a quarter past.'

'Nope,' he says positively. 'Quarter to. You'll hear the god-damn siren in a few minutes, ma'am, five minutes. Three blasts. You'll hear.'

'Personally I think he's wrong,' the teacher says to the girl, in what she considers a confidential undertone, which however I can hear and which the man can also obviously hear, for he barks out a contemptuous one-note laugh.

In the same supposedly secretive voice, the teacher says, 'I overheard what you were saying about that person's petition!' She has inclined her head to the left, so I understand she refers to Havana's petition, not Handle-bars'. She is suddenly off on a fierce lecture on male smoking habits. Cancer and emphysema are not her bug-aboos; a certain kind of slovenliness is—male droppings.

80

The stink of abandoned, damp, chewed cigar butts; the debris of pipes; ash and grains of tobacco strewn on tables and ground into carpets; holes burned in jackets and the laps of others' clothing. 'You just can't sit next to a man with a pipe. . . .' Men and the mouths of men and the foul hot assumptions that come out of the mouths of men.

How much did she hear of what the girl was murmuring to me about her night sorrows? What has ever happened to this teacher in the dark? In the broad daylight a policeman shouts and shouts in her classroom. It seems to me that she asked the girl the time a few minutes ago just for want of something to say, because she is lonely. She suffers the friction of moving pedestrians on her right; her breath is pressed out of her by the line. There is no loneliness like this of hers, almost smothered as she is by flesh.

I have often been lonely in a crowd. I am a somewhat solitary person. But I have discovered something in the petition line—that to be lonely is not the same as to have a distance from people. Loneliness suffocates; one feels the pressure of many bodies; the crowd closes in and crushes one. But when one gets to know one's neighbors enough to see how strange each one of them is, then a bit of space opens up between oneself and them; the pressure eases; the opposite of loneliness—a discriminating intimacy—becomes possible for the first time.

The siren gives out its cry of anguish at the passage of time. Three wails.

The teacher says to the girl in her confidential tone, 'You see? I *said* it was a quarter to. I *knew* he was wrong.'

How LOST I am! A quarter to what?

There are so many distractions. How can I isolate pure feeling from this rush of impressions? I want to savor my gratitude to the girl, which I feel as a tension between the melancholy pain in my chest and a joyful lightheadedness, for her effort to be honest with me, but I feel the janitor's dangerous nose chopping at my ear, and I see the teacher's shoulder in the brown rep dress jerk as she shrugs off the grossness of the cigar man, and I smell the garlic again, see the immobility, now, of the blue pompon, hear the birds in the great cages in the Green, think of the possibility of little Robert poring over a primer. In a minute's time a thousand pictures of heads and parts of heads in the waitline—a red ear, a stray lock, a jaw at work, an eyebrow lifted in disbelief—enter my brain, to be deposited there and held for the day or night

82

when they will be cut up and rearranged and shown as never-before-seen pictures in future inaccurate memories and creative dreams.

I HAVE AN immutable past. I am stuck with it. I cannot exchange it for the past of the man with the red ear, the woman with the lifted eyebrow; mine is there behind me, attached like a cat's tail to my backsides, and to no one else's. It is part of me. This street teems with pasts, many of which I might rather have than my own, but I have mine.

The time will come—I trust it will—when, hoping to pry open a new kind of future, I will share my past with this girl in front of me. We will sit on the edge of my bed in my space and, kicking our heels on the chest, amid all the clatter and fuss of the sleeping-hall—the girl student with two braids typing in the next space, the old head-scratcher up the line with his tummy TV tuned to a game, the pair of squat, dark-skinned women at the foot end of my space gossiping, as they do day and night—I will speak to her about my past in a low voice. I will look straight into her eyes (what color are they? how far apart are they?), and I will say that I want to tell her everything, but I will soon catch myself lying.

83

When I was a boy, anyone could learn to read. . . .
Now this anyway is true: One evening, in Howe Street,
on the way home from orchestra practice, I sneaked my
left hand into the panties of a girl named Marion. I de-
spised her after that. . . . My father tried to teach me to
play chess, but his twitching fingers, reaching for the little pawns and rooks, knocked the larger pieces over, the
kings, queens, and knights. I wept with anger. . . .
While I was working at Sears I stole a blender and gave it
to my mother as a birthday gift. . . .

No, it's no use! Small confessions do not add up to
someone who is special.

I wish I could weave a web of memories of my mother's acts of kindness, my father's aspirations: Those essen-
tials escape me, they are vaporous and indistinct.

I hear instead the sound of a music box—*La ci darem
la mano* . . . The tinkling conjures up a space and an atmosphere. We were twenty. My friend had met a girl he
wanted to try. It was our third year of labor duty, and we
were bunked in what had been built as a school gymnasium—steel trusses overhead, an echoing space; someone
owned that music box. Our arms ached with good physical weariness. My friend asked me if I would switch
bunks with him for one night, as mine was against a wall
and he thought he would make out better in it than in his

84

own, islanded out on the floor. When I think of the silvery sound of the music box—at the moment when Zerlina sighs, '*Andiam! Andiam!*'—I can clearly see the girl's face afterward; it had not been a success, she blamed herself, said she was 'built wrong.' She was mine for the asking.

Perhaps I could talk about *Don Giovanni* with this girl in front of me, when we sit on the edge of my bed, kicking our heels against the chest. *Rosenkavalier. Otello.* But all the talk about music would only encode memories of desire, of attempts to take from strangers whatever I could get at any given moment.

Aɴᴅ ʏᴇᴛ I remain sure that even in this jammed New Haven I am capable of fidelity, of steadfastness toward some as-yet-unknown right person. My life is a search. A glimpse, from the side and behind, of a cheek that is not tense—a whole realm of possibilities! I know objectively what a good meld is. I can tell in two minutes whether a husband and wife are in tune with each other. My mother nursed my ill father for twenty-two years and adored him all that time. She combed the drugstores to find agar-agar leaves for his constipation and admired him with all her heart. They were equals. I never heard a raised voice.

85

I do not mean to feel sorry for myself, but it was easier for them than it is for me. When they were alive, there was room for walls within houses. They seldom had to stand on queues for long—really only when they wanted to see exceptionally good movies.

All these hundreds of thousands of pictures of heads and parts of heads going into my brain in waitlines every day—my search is so fragmentary, so distraught.

'By the way,' I say out loud to the girl, 'what's your name?'

I HAVE ALWAYS believed that a person's name is an aspect of his temperament. It has to be—it was chosen by those who passed on the genetic information and set the daily tone. Call someone by the wrong name and like a mugger you run off with his personality. How incredibly careless! I have stood here against this girl four hours and have begun to mull over issues of loyalty and stability, and I don't even know her name.

She says something, but the janitor sneezes, spraying my cheek, and I cannot hear her words. She waits to see whether he is a two-sneeze or a three-sneeze man.

Atchew! . . . That seems to be all. A two-sneezer. Wet. Hostile to me in his paroxysm.

86

'Maisie.'

I am going to have to adjust my sights as I peer again at the fuzz at the back of her neck. I'll think about that name. I suddenly know all sorts of new things about this girl.

Now I resort again to whispering. 'Why did you laugh when you learned that my name is Sam?'

'I was happy. I've never known man, dog, or cat named Sam that anyone disliked.'

She knows what she is doing. 'Oh,' I say, with the cheap modesty of someone who for a moment can afford it, 'lots of people dislike me.'

'No, Sam,' she says out loud. That just about does it.

I HAVE NEVER liked being sneezed on, and I am feeling a stab of hostility of my own. I have a perfect right to enter any petition I want to. I am not frivolous, as the grandmother is, out here on the line to overcome her boredom. I am not absurd, as Handlebars is. . . .

'I hope that was just hay fever,' I say to the janitor. 'I'd hate to catch a summer cold from you.'

Under attack the janitor at first looks hungry again. I almost break out laughing at the look of a famished hound dog on his face, with its big nose and triangular hound bags under its mournful, close-together hound eyes.

'It's the heat,' he says. 'I get hot, makes me sneeze.'

But then I see the blood drain from his face. He hates the hint of apology in what he has just said to me. His hunger is anger.

My thoughts are still distracted: my cat tail; a new name to fit a person into; daydreams of a future, in which heels kick against furniture; and now at the edge of my mind a bee buzzing, the danger of a bad sting to which I may be allergic.

Perhaps I have made a mistake to turn on the janitor about his miserable pair of sneezes. He is terribly angry. My petition for more space is, it seems, almost unbearably threatening to him. I would guess that he does not dare to think how much he wants what I want. He may be, besides, one of those people who is oversensitive to the constant physical pressure of a waitline; he gets it from me on his left, the pedestrians on the right who, as he complains, have futzed up his whole right arm, the schoolteacher in front of him, and the toucher of my touchers behind him, about whom I have so far found out nothing—a stocky black woman who constantly sighs and says, 'Oh, my,' and 'F-f-f-f-f,' and 'Whoo-o-o-o.'

88

As to space, when I think of it, the janitor is not too badly off. Each night he is alone on staircases. The work may not be pleasant, but he has hours of solitude in echoing stairwells. He is on his knees, facing the upward reach of risers and treads. There is a sense of fluidity about a stairwell; it goes somewhere, aspires, turns on itself and goes up and up. A very good space for a man alone. What more does he want? What a superbly solitary job!

But all he can think of, apparently, is his stacked-up home—two people's belongings in a single person's space, with the rocking chair on top.

Perhaps on his knees at night on the stairs he is tormented; can think of nothing but what has made the steps dirty in this million-footed city. In his ears: scuff, scuff, scuff. I have been stuck in waitline crowds on stairways. I can imagine what he can imagine. Maybe as he swabs foot-filth his imagination never lets him be alone on the stairs; the city's feet kick at his wet hands.

Now he says, squinting, so that anger seems to come in two flattened jets through the constricted nozzles of his eyes, 'I'm going to let all these people know what your petition is.' His nose chops; I see clearly what he means by 'these people.'

I say coolly, 'Why don't you mind your own business?' But I am not sure that I have succeeded in hiding my alarm. He is a leader of chants. I remember the odor of his armpit; and the look of his clenched hands beating out the rhythm for many of us.

S TRANGE THAT I should have imagined the leaves on the maples in the Green whispering, 'Forest, forest, *brother* leaf!' For two generations there has been no such thing as a brother—or a sister. One child only, if any, to a family. My ideas of fraternity—like those of peasantry, royalty, slavery—are all literary. I have a peculiar book-ish fantasy now, that the janitor and I are brothers. We are brothers in a brief passage on the bitter side of our tie. Without himself having any real interest in the girl, he resents my whispering with her. For my part I have a brother's dismay at seeing in him traits that are also sure-ly mine; I want them not.

In my imagination: I am the older brother. Perhaps mimicking my father, I have tried to teach him to play chess, but the first time I checked his king he lost his tem-per and knocked over the board.

In my imagination: His name is Cain. My flesh creeps.

90

Yes, my flesh moves. I cannot call this anything so ugly now as lust. I feel a justifying tenderness.

My irritation at the janitor and my deep fear of a brother's wrath are, for some reason, aphrodisiac. I am a little bit thrilled by the hunger on my right.

I have only been in a fight once. I did not like it. It was while I was on labor duty. We were laying concrete. I was aiming the chute from the mixer into the form. I pushed too hard. A big gob of the mix fell outside the form and buried the foot of my friend who had traded bunks with me. He accused me of doing it on purpose. We became angry. There was much daring of each other to cross an invisible line; in this we were like small boys. But then the blows began, and we were like men. Like grown brothers—out to kill. I gritted my teeth; he boxed my chin and I saw stars. He choked me until I began to pass out. But his nose was bleeding afterward, and his cheek was black and blue. Who had won? That night I scored with his girlfriend; she was not 'built wrong' at all.

The memory of cheating my friend, of the way in which the afternoon's anger, fear, courage, and pain were converted into the night's overwhelming gentleness, are strongly with me now.

91

Our loss of control by the concrete mixer that afternoon brought us a severe penalty. Our labor duty was extended by six months. Can I make myself think of penalties now?

I remember seeing an old film of two mountain goats, rams with huge curling horns, charging at each other over and over with booming collisions, to settle which would enjoy the ready ewe. We two friends weren't like that; no one had 'won.' Clear still pictures of the rams linger in my mind—he-goats, raunchy aggressors, their hind legs the legs of the satyr. . . . I remember that the Greek word for tragedy means goat's song. . . . Had that to do with hairy nether parts?—burnt sacrifices?—the music Pan made?

All that holds me in check, I think, is the thought that the girl has had to invent a face for me. What if it is the face of the man she lost?

I NOW BELIEVE I am going to reach the windows this morning. I am less than a hundred feet from the arched doorways.

The closer we get to the bureau building, the tighter the line is packed. The grandmother, disgusted that she

92

cannot strike up a satisfying conversation, is red in the face and is breathing with some difficulty.

The cloth that separates me from Maisie is soaked with perspiration; the dampness between us is not unpleasant.

Here in the beginning of the shadow of the bureau building there is more excitement around us. The cigar man is talking in nervous bursts—not at all as my father used to talk. The fullness under his jaw shakes with each humorous thrust. He is trying to get Maisie's attention.

I am also aware of Handlebars' voice, which has a droning yet penetrating quality. He is talking to the painter about his memory of the taste of a certain cheese made in New York State; he dwells at length on the remembered sensation of the cheese dissolving in his mouth, the interplay of taste and touch on his tongue.

All around us there is quick chatter. Hope bubbles up as we approach the windows. The pompon bobs.

A sturdy woman off to the left, beyond the cigar man, throws her head back to laugh; the mass of her hair squashes into the face of a totally bald man behind her, who shakes his head back and forth and spits to get hairs out of his mouth. He protests cheerfully. Was she laughing at a joke of his? I look closely at his face to see whether I can detect signs of his having developed a relationship with the woman against whom he is pressed by the waitline. He has liver blotches on his skin, and a bumpy nose like a gnarl on a maple tree. What does the woman imagine he looks like?

The painter still croaks out his urgings. 'Come on, come on, come *on!*' he shouts. Here near the doors his voice now has a resolute ring.

Each time he barks, the black woman beside him and behind the janitor makes one of her sounds of tested patience. I sense that she is carrying on a teasing game with the painter; making wild eyes; she is unable to believe there could be anyone so ill-equipped to stand and wait.

All these impressions of rising excitement, together with countless new pictures of bits of heads in the line—a pierced ear with a gold circlet hanging from it, a greenish-purplish bruise like a slice of an unripe plum, the beginnings of a goiter, a woman's hairy upper lip—enter my mind at its fringes. They are all distractions. In the middle ground of my attention, at the point where the rays of sunlight through the lens converge to set things on fire, there are only the janitor's warning and the definite encouragement I now think I am getting from Maisie. All the excitement around us is drawn down to this hot, ambiguous point.

94

4

LIKE A NAGGING younger brother the janitor hisses, 'But it *is* my business. I might be next to you at the windows. It *is* my business.'

Fire is in the back of my mind.

Before my father's hands began to shake, he made exquisitely realistic cardboard and wooden models of boats and airplanes and racing cars for me. I marveled at his skill with those hands, which had black hairs on the

95

backs of the fingers between the knuckles. As I grew older and he slid into his illness, I came to love the surface textures of the cheap violin he had bought me, its graceful neck and scroll, its ebony pegs, the sweep of the *f*-hole, the powerful architecture of the fragile bridge; and in my envy of his former skill I dreamed of making something more marvelous than he had ever made—a real violin. One day I read in the back pages of a comic book about an eccentric tinkerer who had made a violin by gluing wooden kitchen matches together in layers. I began to glue up some of my mother's matches. When she came home from shopping she was panicked by the heaps of blue-tipped match heads that had accumulated after the first hour; I was saving them to make little homemade fireworks, of the sort we called torpedoes, by wrapping them in tight little packages mixed with grit. She screamed when she saw the match heads on the table and floor—the only scream I ever heard from that gentle and serene woman. She forbade me to work with matches, and I was saved from the humiliation of my father's laughter, which I would surely have earned when he eventually found out what I was trying to make, and with what materials.

The crux of this memory has come and gone in an instant. The janitor is still after me. 'I was talking to you,'

96

he says. 'Listen,' he says, 'I could turn you in, the way you're fooling around.' His nose, which serves for an index finger now that his arms are pinned to his sides, points at Maisie.

'I am *not* fooling around,' I say. 'Ask her.'

I have put myself ridiculously on the defensive. I have let his charge get under my skin. Brotherlike, he immediately realizes his advantage. 'I got eyes,' he says.

'They don't see so well.'

'I'm not deaf.'

'I told you before. Mind your own business.'

'I told you before—the thing you're going to ask for, it *is* my business. You're not going to put in for that.'

'I have a right to enter any petition I want.'

'Oh, brother!' he exclaims, raising his eyes to the sky. His casual use of this everyday expression of outrage frightens me more than any threat he has made up to now.

But what he says next restores my anger right away—and my desire. 'I'm going to make sure,' he says, 'that you don't get to those windows.'

97

My ANGER and my desire are hand in hand. Both need space. To fight, to make love—a ring, a bower. In a fleeting fantasy I have plenty of room to wind up and throw a haymaker and I hear that rudder of a nose on the janitor's face crack like wood, and at the same instant I have put my hands gently on Maisie's shoulders and have turned her around facing me, and in a capsule of privacy I pull her body close to mine.

In reality she has heard what the janitor has said. She turns her head to the left and murmurs, 'How *can* you justify what you're asking for?'

It is not that she is on the janitor's side; I understand that. She does not know what the janitor plans to do to keep me from the windows; whatever he says or does, she wants me to have a strong case. Her question is solicitous. I translate it: She really means she wants me to turn her around and hug her. I am not so afraid now as I was earlier of the consequences of breaking the law.

In my mind space is positive. Some people make space for themselves by holding themselves aloof. Half closing their eyes, which bright light hurts, they see others through a distorting, rainbow-tinted film of their own eyelashes, and they think loud thoughts in order not to hear what their neighbors are saying. Theirs is negative space. For me space gives, derives from, and *is* peace of mind. One has to make it for himself. One has to seek it, strive for it, if necessary fight for it—certainly ask for it.

'I need it,' I answer Maisie. 'I'll never get it by waiting for it to come to me.'

'That's not going to satisfy *them.*'

The grandmother is laughing; I feel her body shaking and her guffaws assail my left ear. She is now very jolly. She has at last found a talker in Handlebars. He has nothing to say to her that hasn't to do with his enjoyment of his six senses—for he seems to have one more than the rest of us, the extra one being seated, evidently, in his glans. His talk is lusty, stupid, and endless, but it finally justifies the grandmother's morning.

A shriek in my right ear shoots terror to my gut. It is the janitor—rage and frustration.

After the cry he shouts at the top of his voice, 'Everybody listen to me! This guy to the left of me! His petition! More space! The son of a bitch is asking for more space in his sleeping-hall!'

THE TEACHER, directly in front of the janitor, starts
and cries out, 'Hoo-oo! You scared me!'

Everyone around me has been alarmed by the loud-
ness of, and the sharp edge on, the janitor's voice. Faces
from ahead all turn to see where the outburst came from.
Many pedestrians, shuffling slowly along against the current of our line, show that they are startled and baffled.
The cigar man looks annoyed.

Maisie groans, 'Oh, no!'

After the first gasps and exclamations there is something like silence—the city's blank roar. This lasts only a
few seconds. Then everyone is talking at once.

The janitor is ecstatic. He has turned his chopper toward me and is muttering, 'There! You see? You bastard.
I told them. Now you're going to see. You wait. Everybody—they know, see? I told them. I told you I was going
to stop you. Didn't I? You bastard, you'll see! You aren't
going to bollix me up. . . .'

The stab of dread that the janitor's first outcry sent
through me put my body on alert. My heart is pounding.
My arms are held tight. My buttocks prickle. I feel a new
energy. The handclasp of my anger and my desire is

100

tightened. The sympathy in Maisie's groan has vibrated in my chest. I am more conscious than ever of my pressure against her. I am breaking the law. I am definitely breaking the law.

My eyes sweep the faces turned our way. The first response is like that of people having heard the first sharp crack of a thunderstorm. There is a primitive reflex—close the windows! get under the beds!—and then anger at the thunder, anger at the assault on the eardrums, anger at the anger in the electric bolt.

The faces are disapproving—of the janitor. I hear shouts. 'Shut up!' 'Pipe down!' 'Go to hell!' 'Hang it up!' Some of those nearest us—the painter behind me, and the teacher in front of the janitor, for two—must remember their outrage at the janitor's own loud complaints about space not long ago, about having all his things moved and stacked up in a single space after he took his wife to Connecticut Valley; I hear the painter now barking, 'Look who's talking!' The teacher, recovered from her start, has resumed her natural habit of disapprobation, with which she now scalds the janitor; she has some skill in this line, and her voice crackles.

Gradually the janitor, his monologue trickling down like a spilt pitcherful to the end of its run, has become aware of this surprising reply to his screams. He looks

101

around. Is suddenly ready for lunch. Begins to swallow air again.

For the second time this morning Maisie is inclining her head back toward mine. She knows what has happened to me. Yes! She is my accomplice now. She will certainly not report me, for after her manner she, too, is breaking the law.

There is so much chatter and turbulence around us that I take a big chance, say out loud to her, 'Wait for me by the windows when you're finished with your petition.'

Her head, still leaning back, almost touching mine, nods ever so slightly.

By the time the janitor has absorbed his surprise at the resentment of the waitline against him, I can see that the feeling of the crowd has already subtly shifted ground. The words he shouted have begun to sink in. *The son of a bitch on my left is asking for more space!*

Only a few—my touchers and their touchers, perhaps—know exactly who the shouter was, and so who the person on the shouter's left is. The eyes from up ahead are searching, searching.

Even as I luxuriate in, am further excited by, the thought of Maisie's nod, I see the change in those eyes and on the faces in which they are set. As alarm has given

102

way to anger, so now anger shifts from accuser to accused. The eyes not only search; they begin to hunt.

Since many do not know who these two are, accuser and accused, the anger is at first abstracted. They are angry at the idea that a person, some son of a bitch on somebody's left, should even think of broaching a forbidden subject at the petition windows. The idea threatens them, they feel their own petitions jeopardized. I know that this is ridiculous—they are ahead of me in the line—but I suppose they do not think of this, such is the repulsive power of the idea.

I look to my right. The janitor is still chewing his meager snack of disappointment. I see that my reading of the crowd's temper has outpaced his. He will soon be happier. With my emotions strongly drawn down toward my breaking of the law, I am nevertheless (or perhaps therefore) clear-headed. My desire has made me hawk-sharp. I know I must build my defenses, prepare a counterattack.

The place to start is close at hand—my touchers, and theirs. These few know who was meant. Maisie is with me. The janitor cannot be brought round. The grandmother—no; I was coy about my petition with her. The painter behind me—morose, fractious, in a blind hurry;

103

yet it was he who made the merciful suggestion of passing the woman who had fainted up to the windows, and I
have just heard him snarl, 'Look who's talking!'

I turn my head around to the left to speak to him,
but as I do so, I wonder what I can really say. The reason
for his impatience with the janitor was precisely that the
janitor had been bitching about space. Yet there does
seem to be some sense of fairness in this sullen man, and I
must try to enlist it.

Can it be that one reason I think of appealing to him
is that I cannot see his face?

I firmly say, 'Anybody's allowed to make any petition he wants. Right?'

Handlebars thinks I am speaking to him. He grins at
me in his goofy way. Since he refers everything to an index of his senses, he has no way of dealing with this kind
of generalization. 'Sure,' he says, 'why not?'

He is a self-centered fool. He will be of no help at all.
I draw my breath to renew my appeal to the painter—
when suddenly everyone around me is talking at once.

I make out the grandmother's reproach: 'So that's
why you didn't want to tell me!' At the moment this is a
harmless rebuke, having more to do with my inadequacy
as a conversationalist than with the substance of my petition. But the Havana-cigar man is looking at me with a

104

shocked expression. 'You?' he says. '*You?*' The teacher, too, is jabbering at me, but I cannot make out her words. I sense that the janitor is, as I predicted he would be, getting high again. The lottery man's head turns from side to side; he is calling out something or other. Beneath the gnarled nose in the liver-spot-splotched face I see a cavern of outrage opening and closing, opening and closing.

Maisie is trying to say something—out loud—but her words seem snatched away by the noise around us, as if she were shouting into a gale of wind. Maisie! I want to slide my hands forward around your hips and clasp you, but the teacher and the cigar man would feel the backs of my hands creeping past their flanks.

The janitor sounds off again at the top of his voice. 'Here he is! On my left! Petition for more space!'

This loud shout knocks back the hubbub again; there is another momentary lull.

Then, as new gusts of sound start up, Maisie says aloud, and I hear her, 'Sam! Couldn't you change your mind?'

I really could not. I feel that I am going to have my turn at shouting. I am going to shout, 'You *all* ought to be asking for more space! What are you afraid of? What have you to lose? Come on! Join me!'

How can I change my mind, when my need under-

105

lies every choice, every action, every gesture of my life? Acceptance is out of the question. I am a writer. I need space. I can almost hear Maisie saying, her voice muffled by kindness, 'But you only write departmental reports.' But I *make* something—something new. I am a writer— an enemy of Acceptance. The painter behind me—*he* must need space. Maisie—she has the female gift of creation that artists can only imitate. Open up! Give her room!

'Did you hear me, Sam?' She, too, is shouting now.

Her concern moves me, charges me with pleasure. Do I imagine that I feel her body moving—her hips? We need more space, more space! I need room to turn her altogether around, or, if not that, we need compass—room to flex and search. My illegality reaches in vain for her generosity. We are pressed from every side.

While pressured this way I cannot budge, either physically or in principle. I am afraid I am stubborn. I am unwilling to accept under duress. If I had more space, perhaps I could be more open to persuasion and change. I am locked in.

'No, Maisie,' I say, using her strange name for the first time, 'I'm sorry to say I can't change my mind.'

There is a great deal of loud, impatient talk around us, but I think I hear her say, 'I'm afraid.'

106

THERE IS A SCRABBLING movement at my right thigh. Once again the janitor is fighting to raise his arms.

I know what this means, and I say quite loudly, 'Knock it off.'

He says, 'You aren't going to those windows.'

'Why are you so upset by somebody asking for more space?'

His hand still struggling for freedom, he shouts, 'You trying to queer it for all of us?'

'But you said you need more space yourself. Your rocking chair . . .'

'Who don't? Who don't?'

I can see that this is no time for reason. There is more and more turbulence around us. The circuitry printer is scolding me in a smothering maternal tone. The teacher badmouths me. Cigars is patronizing, Handlebars is jocular. I have heard nothing from the painter or from the black woman beside him. But these, my touchers and some of my touchers' touchers, know me as a more or less real person. I realize that a much more unsparing hostility comes from farther out in the line, where I am nothing but a notion—a nonperson with an irresponsible urge to be a spoiler.

M<small>Y</small> FIRST EXPERIENCES of women, apart from
that thirty-seven-year-old in caftan with zipper, were
while I was on labor duty, in the former gym, where men
and women workers were housed together at random. I
never knew sex that had no audience. All my generation
grew up both actors in, and viewers of, a whole-life movie. My parents clung to an old-fashioned sense of privacy; so long as we had a room of our own, and before my
father's illness was far advanced, they stole moments together when I was out; I never saw Father wrestling
with Mother. I came into possession of the facts of life
when I was seven, my informant an older man of nine.
Graphic details were easy to come by. By the time I was
eleven I had a thirty-seven-year-old's 'experience' of sex,
I had 'done' and 'seen' everything, normal acts and their
variants—all in my head; and on my daybed by night I
had fantasies, for a short time, that that other wrestler
would quietly choke my father to death, and my mother
would creep under the covers with me and teach me all
that I already knew; with incestuous charity she would
move the bank of my experience from my cranium to my
scrotum. She would be capable of instructing me in extremely nice activities, and in extremely naughty ones.

108

Many of my friends, their parents more modern than mine, had received exemplary teaching. History tells us that we have long been a nation of watchers. My first lessons in that gym were visual. Up to that time I had groped; I was immature; only the blind can see with their fingertips. I think I had caught a certain anachronistic fastidiousness from my parents. But sex in public—consummation on one cot, conversation on the next—was such a commonplace, 'trying' friends and friends of friends among friends was so matter-of-course, sharing and trading and seeing and touching and switching and not waiting were all so usual that I was soon in the swim—skinny-dipping in a sensuous sea of trial and error. With my generation, on which proximity forced early visual intimacies, something strange happened: The eyes hardened. One who too often handles hard things gets calluses on his hands; many of us who too often saw sweet things got scales on our eyes. And with the dulling of sight came a deadening of feeling, both in the fingertips and in the soul. I was perhaps a little bit different. This may be why I am special. I can still be surprised and thrilled by what I see. I am a writer. Powerful emotions are wired to my eyes. *This* is why I need space: I have to see sometimes at middle and long range. I cannot be forever thrilled and cross-eyed. It is all very well that my first

109

sight of Maisie, one that enlisted something more than curiosity in me, was of the disorderly baby-fine curls at the back of her neck. Now that that something more has so quickly been mobilized, now that she and I are conspiring together to break the law, I need desperately to stand back and see her whole.

I heard Maisie's challenge about my responsibility for the break-up with my wife. Was my wife's problem about having sex under others' eyes something I somehow foisted on her, as I made the effort to free myself of the need for privacy which I had somehow caught from my out-of-step parents?

How do I know that Maisie does not have hard eyes? It does not seem to matter to her whether my face is a face in a novel or one in a film. To her, it seems, a face is a face—just an interchangeable oval something. My need for space includes a need to be seen whole, myself, and of course then to be recognized.

To those who do not see me, I am a spoiler. How wrong they are!

But perhaps all those who do not see me have hard eyes, anyway, and can only see what they choose to see —have eyes which seem to see what is actually there but which distort, which substitute stale images for fresh ones, which blur and confuse and then convince; and

110

which play these tricks because for so very long nothing has been hidden.

D<small>ESPITE THE FIERCE</small> crowd pressure here near the head of the line, the janitor manages to get his hands up, and, beating the air like a mad conductor, he starts a new chant.

'Get out of the line! Get out of the line! Get out of the line! Get out of the line! . . .'

He shouts this command, looking at me, his nose slicing the morning, half a dozen times before a single other voice takes it up. Then some others join in, here one, there another. The first few to chime in are at some distance from us. Apart from him, none of my touchers or touchers' touchers gives voice.

Maisie turns her head and, her cheek twisted, shouts to the janitor, 'Stop it! Stop it!'

I sense that she is trying to push outward with her arms, against the teacher and the cigar man. Is this because the janitor's chant has frightened her, and she needs more room to inhale the breath of fear, or is she trying somehow to make space for us? Below her waist she has given me signals that she knows, and accepts, my delinquency.

111

She has tried to sandwich her shouts of protest between the sentences of the chant. But nothing can stop the janitor now. His eyes, with only the bundleboard of the nose between them, are inflamed, passionate. He thinks he has the ump where he wants him now.

Any crowd is like dry grass to the flames of any rhythmic cry, and this fire quickly spreads. There is not the exuberance this time that there was in the shouts on behalf of the woman who had fainted. That was a rescue; we cheered her up the line; there was a bubble of laughter under the sound in each throat. Now the janitor's voice beside me is a croak; the chant is dreary in its viciousness.

I see the fullness under the jaw of the cigar man begin to pulse in time with the janitor's arms. Too bad; he has gone over. Does he have any idea what the movements beside his right arm and thigh mean? I have seen him look at Maisie once or twice, his eyes like bits drilling into her intentions. Does he think that she is trying to nestle closer to *him?*

He is shouting with a full throat, 'Get out of the line! Get out of the line! . . .'

The grandmother screams at me, a motherly tenderness in her eyes, 'Why didn't you tell me?' Does she think

112

she could have spared me this trouble—if only I had been a talker?

Maisie has given up trying to silence the janitor. She is shaking her head slowly. Down there—she *must* know the law. . . .

I hear Handlebars' penetrating drone now, in phase with the rhythm. He would join in any movement that promised satisfaction of any kind; perhaps he just likes to shout.

Nothing yet from the painter.

I wonder if they could really force me out of the line. Everyone knows I have a right to be on it. *They* are breaking the law. Mob action in waitlines is far more cruelly punished than, say, a man's indiscretion toward a blonde with wispy curls at the back of her neck. The chanters are conspiring in a gross felony. Should I warn the janitor? . . . It would do no good. He is at the mercy of an impulse nothing could stop now. He has a hurtling terror of wanting anything as much as he wants space.

H E HAS CHANGED the shout. Now he barks out just one word, over and over and over: 'Out! . . . Out! . . . Out! . . . Out! . . . Out! . . .'

113

The abbreviation catches on.

Now much of the line is engaged. Crowd transcendence has set in. The mere rhythm, without any content or meaning, grips each person, lifts each person out of his skin and into the soul of the crowd. Of those near me, only the girl and the grumpy painter are silent now. The grandmother rocks her head back and forth with each shout. I see that many of the pedestrians, who have no idea what this is about, have taken up this simpler rhythm: 'Out! . . . Out! . . . Out! . . .' The blue pompon on the red cap sharply bobs with each explosion. Into the memory bank in my brain go stretching jaws, mouths around the *ow* sound, pumping cowlicks, a dance of ears.

It occurs to me that if I am forced out of the line I may never see Maisie again.

I lean down to her ear and shout, 'Where do you live?'

She seems to understand, turns her head, shouts something which is swallowed into the rhythmic noise. For a horrible moment I think she is shouting, 'Out!'

'I can't hear!'

She turns her head and screams three words, and this time I do hear: 'Change your mind!'

114

Sʜᴏᴜʟᴅ I? I wonder now: Should I?

Her meaning is not the janitor's. She is not thinking of herself. I trust she is thinking of me. Perhaps I can believe that she is selfish in the sense that she may want a future relationship with me; she may not want the object of that relationship to be in danger. This object does not yet have a face, but it has an expressed value below the belt. Yes. . . . Yes. . . . Yes. . . .

Out! . . . *Out!* . . . *Out!* . . . *Out!* . . . *Out!* . . . *Out!* . . .

The crowd in the line is mindless now. It has a single pulse and a single need—a scapegoat. Tragedy—the scapegoat's song?

The reason I wonder whether I should change my mind has to do, in the first instance, with Maisie. If she can think of me, I can also think of her. Will my petition endanger hers? The grandmother says she has no chance anyway. But supposing she presents her case well; supposing I am at the next window; supposing the official anger really is of the sort the janitor has imagined. . . .

I am capable of thinking beyond Maisie to others in the line. Desire is expansive; infatuation opens out horizons. Or, to put the thought in its frankest form (some think frankness honesty): One who feels lust is not cut off from others. Desire has made me resemble my mother. I am suddenly charitable. Will I endanger the petitions of others besides Maisie? Proteins, Havanas, a skill, a baby, a lottery . . . Strange! I don't know what the petition is of the one person I think of as an ally, besides Maisie—the grump behind me, *still* not chanting. Do I want to endanger whatever it is he wants?

But a selfish thought, after all, wins out. I shout again in Maisie's ear, 'Where do you live?' I do not want to lose her.

This is the first time in my life I have had a person's address screamed at me. In the midst of all my distraction I try to chisel it into my memory: 240 Park Street. Has Maisie enough space? Surely not!

I am on the point of changing my mind.

Not that I care about the threat of the chant. It excites me. I am not only charitable; I am enlarged.

Bad questions: Would it do any good to change my mind? Could I make myself heard? Even if I did, would that make any difference? Does this crowd want a sacrifice more than it wants an idea? Give the janitor an inch—will he want a mile? Does he hate me now more than my petition?

116

I nevertheless decide to shout at him between *outs.* I think I will accede. My mouth is open.

A scream. Match heads.

It almost seems as if the tearing scream is coming out of my own mouth.

It is so frightful that I cannot tell whether it causes or comes from the fear I feel.

I recognize at once what it is. It is line-sickness. Danger.

It goes on and on. It cuts right through the crowd-shout. It is behind me.

5

I S IT THE PAINTER, who has not taken part in the chant? Has he been trying with all his strength to hold himself together? Is it he?

There is a metallic edge to the scream.

Already my touchers, and theirs, and theirs, have stopped shouting. The janitor's arms are still pumping, but his throat seems to have dried up.

My desire has fled; tenderness remains. Maisie, like

everyone else, must be afraid. I want more than ever to enfold her—to lessen my own fear by showing my concern for hers.

Now I recognize that sound of brass in the held shriek. It is not in the painter's voice. This comes from the neck of the young man with the mustache. The metallic sound is an enlargement, by a hundredfold, of the penetrating, boring sound of his hedonism which I heard earlier.

I see the panic on the grandmother's face—she who makes parties out of waitlines. The scream is right behind her.

The cigar man's head jerks from side to side.

Line-sickness is so catching. If rhythm can spread like fire in a crowd, this can explode. A sick line is a writhing mass of the damned.

The scream has been going on for only about ten seconds, but already I can barely hear in the distance: *Out! . . . Out! . . . Out! . . .*

The janitor is no longer pumping. He cannot get his arms down. He holds them up, like a man who has lost his will and wants to surrender.

STRANGE THAT it should be Handlebars who could not bear waiting any longer. He has seemed to have such a thick skin. Are the selfish after all most vulnerable? No, that is too easy. There are kinds and kinds of selfishness. His is all sensory. Also, he is a particular sort of hedonist: a stupid hedonist. His dreary drone; his feathery mustaches—he has constructed a face for himself, perhaps a whole character for himself, out of a Zamport movie, one of those memory-Westerns. But the film has suddenly slipped off the sprockets of the projector, the sound track is horribly askew.

THE SCREAM goes on and on. The *out*-chant has died. The crowd has forgotten the spoiler. Every one of us is holding on tight. Each knows that if he—or his neighbor—gives way, then another more easily gives way; the chain reaction starts.

If it must be known, none of us can bear any of this any longer.

My own alarm, terrible as it is, *is* abated by my con-

121

cern for Maisie. How can I get a message of comfort or of courage to her? Words would not penetrate the scream-tone. Can I take the risk of moving my hands? Would it help her if I did?

My view of the line ahead is of rigidity. Each person, eyes front, holds his head firmly in place, as if by immobility to lock the wild beast of the line-sickness out of his skull.

Handlebars seems never to take a breath; his scream somehow eternally renews itself. His pain, from being crowded too long, is hideous. His is the blatant, penetrating, awry, monotonous rage of a stuck bus horn.

The pedestrians no longer move. No pedestrian's face looks our way. Heads are held stiffly toward the Green.

Are the birds silent in the great cages?

The traffic has stopped.

The entire morning has seized up. We are figures in a photograph.

There *is* motion. I feel Maisie's body trembling.

I slowly slide my flat hands forward—we are so hard pressed that it takes all my strength—and I grasp her hips. Her head droops back toward mine. Good! My solicitude becomes strength and pours into her flanks through my palms.

122

The back of a hand is against the back of my left hand. I see the cigar man's head make a quarter turn to the right, but the wind of the scream soon blows it back straight again.

T HE TEACHER breaks. A second siren in a second throat, this one higher-pitched.

Danger! Danger! Not twice as great as before: a thousand times greater.

I can see the teacher's face lifted to send up to the sky, like a factory's pollution, all the poison of all the years of her disapprobation, forced out of her now by her being so sick of this crowd-pressure. Her throat is swollen; it can hardly contain the fund of the scream yet to come.

T HERE IS A NEW sound. Under the horrible harmonic fifth of the two screams it seems far away. Yet it is near me, too.

Is it the beginning of a third scream in a third larynx nearby?

123

It is louder now. It is behind me. It is the painter. He is singing.

I recognize the song—a strange song that has been popular lately, a corrupted lullaby, commonly sung to a rather crisp and even danceable tune. There are so few children allowed now that real lullabies are no longer current; this song is a queer relic. It seems to me to have odd subliminal elements from some alienated culture of long ago—surely the baby who is being lulled is not tiny; it strikes me that it may be in its teens. Amazing that the painter would know this song! What he does know—has remembered before any of the rest of us—is that if anything can hold a line together when these screams freeze the air, it is singing.

Another voice has taken up the song—that of the black woman to the painter's right; a huge, orotund contralto tone of hymn-singing habit, wishful, mournful, visionary, knowing hell, yearning for what has so long been promised: another land, another way.

Now, of all people, the janitor joins in, *fortissimo.*

The big ear-ripping fifth still goes on. Others are beginning to hear the song and take it up. Both Maisie and I do. The grandmother belts it out.

Now the janitor's arms are pumping again to the fast beat of the song:

124

Cry, little beebee, cry if you will.
Rock and split and dip and roll.
Sleep, little beebee, sleep if you can;
Mum's up in crumbtown holding your hand.
Mum's in the cakehouse; sleep, sleep.
Bread's in the bank, dear; drip, drip.
Suck . . . suck . . . suck . . . suck . . .
Cry, little beebee, cry if it spills.
Sleep, little beebee, down a downer.
Cry, little beebee, sleep, sleep.

All along the line voices take hold of the song.

I AM AMAZED by the janitor, leading the song to save us all—including *me*. Is he some kind of idiot who just cannot help waving his arms when any repitition offers itself? No, no, it is more than that. His nose is slicing up and down, a baton of hope; his dog eyes encourage me. 'Sing! Sing!' the eyes say. It comes to me that he is the sort of human being who will survive. He will survive anything. Storm, famine, mob, war, massacre, pressure of numbers. In order to survive, he will with even-handed

125

equanimity destroy and rescue. Partner and enemy, chopper and baton, coward and hero—he conducts equally well on alternating and direct current. I think now that I could despise him even if he hadn't put me in mortal danger. Look at the happy little eyes encouraging his brother to sing!

The screams persist, but the lullaby blankets us—a fire-fighters' foam.

The painter is something else. As I roar the song I remember how his crankiness annoyed me at first. I did not want any part of knowing him. How often in my life I have misjudged people!

I KEEP LISTENING for a third scream. The sound goes round and round. Without actually realizing it at the time of doing it, I have pushed my hands farther forward; my left forearm crosses uncomfortably between the Havana man's arm and Maisie's hip. She is now singing loud. I know that I am inwardly safe now, despite being bracketed by the two continuing screams; and I believe, from the way her throat swells with the lullaby, that Maisie is safe, too, even though one of the screams is right beside her.

126

Mum's in the cakehouse, sleep, sleep . . .

I hear the painter now shouting at the top of his voice to Handlebars, who is screaming beside him. 'It's all right!' the painter roars. 'We're almost there! Ten minutes! Look at the doors! It's okay! We're almost to the doors!' And soon, like a noon siren winding down at the end of its high-pitched shriek, Handlebars' sickness leaves him on a dying fall.

Now there is just the one scream. I take the painter's cue and shout soothing encouragements to the teacher. Her trouble is stubborn, but I know that thanks to the song the waitline as a whole is safe.

The high hot wind in the teacher's frame finally spends itself, and the sound in her throat climbs down to a long groan, and then to nothing. The song is drawn into the vacuum her quiet makes, and it, too, gradually subsides.

WHAT A LUXURY silence is!

127

IT IS A TRANSIENT luxury. A general buzzing begins. The pedestrians and the traffic move again.

So does Maisie, ever so slightly, under my hands. I
am surprised by the sudden return of my prodigal desire;
it has come riding in on my relief. Yes, I am having reason to be surprised, and not only by its alacrity. My in-
fraction is impressive.

But now I am drawn aside: 'All I ask,' the janitor
says to me, his expression now quite friendly, 'is, you
don't stand at the next window to me.' He talks in an
even voice, as if nothing at all unusual has been happening.

'I don't know if I can have any control over that.'

'Sure you can. Look, when we go through the doors,
there's a rush, see, for these turnstiles. You ever been
here?'

'Not actually to the windows.'

'Okay, they have these turnstiles, the police control
them. They let you through the doors to go inside when
one of the turnstiles in there is empty. So all you have to
do is, when we go through the doors, you rush to the left,
I rush to the right.'

'I'll try.'

128

'It's a deal.'

What interests me is not that the janitor has decided against resuming his effort to keep me from the windows—probably he is aware that once line-sickness has broken out and been controlled, it remains dangerously close beneath the surface—but rather that I have decided to go ahead with my petition.

The cigar man is looking at me in a peculiar way.

WE REALLY ARE approaching the Romanesque arches in the dark brick wall. Before the doors there are two steps up, then a landing. There is a police barrier on the landing just outside the doors. The uniformed men let people through two or three at a time—that is obviously when the rush comes.

I know I should be thinking of what I will say at the window. But as usual I am distracted. The painter is consoling Handlebars, who is abjectly apologetic. The teacher is weeping. Oddly, it is the seedy lottery man who is trying to comfort her over the right shoulder of his bush jacket. The grandmother is pleased; she hasn't had such an entertaining morning in a month of rest days. How much to talk about! 'Right behind me! Like he was being stuck with an ice pick!' The janitor is trying to tell

129

me that he is the one who pulled us all through, by leading the song; he thinks maybe the authorities will take that into account as they hear his petition. Would I mind mentioning it? Has he already forgotten that he wants as much distance as possible between us?

Yes, Maisie now knows that the prodigal is home. Once again her head leans back toward mine. But my great pleasure now is not sensory; it is my enjoyment of what she and I share: a secret event.

Or is it a secret? Havana is still staring at me. He looks as if he is trying to decide whether to make a purchase.

And all the while, fragmentary images of waiting humanity enter my distracted brain. I see a wart, a wen, a blackened tooth, a bent nose and a blue lip, a roll of fat at the back of a neck, a hairy ear, a satin cheek, greedy eyes, a too-neat pair of dark braids, a balding crown, a sag in a jowl, a pain-line at the edge of a mouth, a dimple, crow's-feet, and pink wriggling veins—scraps of hope, bits of revealed struggle, signs here and there that it is already too late.

THE LINE IS one long held breath. False notes that have been coming from the janitor, of friendliness, of ap-

130

peal, are in key with the hung mood of the whole wait-line. Everyone has the sense of having narrowly missed going over the waterfall, there is great relief; but wariness, too. People are speaking words they don't mean. Being so close to the arched doorways gives all of us at the front of the line a giddy, unready feeling. I see the cops on the steps at the doors, dressed in the dark blue of our social contract, and I can even hear their voices, which in their way are in uniform, too: the sound is clean, well pressed, and buttoned up, and like neat dark cloth it makes respectable the impulse to crime in the crime-fighter. 'You next. . . .' 'Okay, ma'am. . . .' 'Hold it up! Not so fast! . . .'

Pompon has reached the steps. Up one. He certainly is a tall man. The back of his shirt is soaked.

'Good luck,' I say out loud to Maisie.

She turns her head and whispers, 'Are you going through with it?'

'Sure,' I say, 'I couldn't not.' I hear the falsehood in my claim. Maisie does not know what I know—that I was on the point, when the *out*-chant was loudest, of changing my mind. I have made myself sound much more steadfast than I have actually been. The screams have shaken me, like everyone else, out of the truth groove.

Will I have regained my balance by the time I go

131

through the turnstiles? I wonder how I am going to start off. I will clear my throat and say, 'My petition is for more space in the sleeping-hall.' That is direct, but it sounds weak. I must assert my right to what I want. I must get across to whoever or whatever is behind the window that I am special. How can I do that, though, in a few sentences? I am not aware that I have succeeded, in more than four hours, in conveying this to Maisie.

WE ARE ALMOST to the doors. My heart beats hard. The lottery man goes up one step. The back of his bush jacket is soaked. Maisie's sweat is mixed there in the expensive whipcord with his.

The grandmother is saying good-bye to her new acquaintances, as if a party were drawing to a close. 'Nice knowing you,' she says to me, seeming to have forgotten the noggin-snapping zest with which she asked for my ouster not many minutes ago. Her eyes are huge, sentimental. 'I live at the Elmhurst, Elm Street, just near the Broadway branch of the First National Bank, you know? Look me up, huh? I make *such* good friends in these lines. I don't know, it seems like people that take the trouble to put in petitions—well, they're special. Really are. You, too, honey,' she says toward Maisie.

132

All these packed people, stretching still back to the corner of Church and Elm and around it down toward Orange—all special? This loose language of the circuitry printer punches my claim in the solar plexus. . . . But she is not with me any more. She is saying over her right shoulder, 'As for *you*, Harry boy. . . .' Harry seems to be Handlebars' name. The grandmother's insensitivity to him, after what he has gone through, is monstrous. Heaving with a sense of fun, she calls him an old card and reminds him of some tired morsel of self-centered porno he tossed off earlier, and she explodes with jollity. Handlebars has made an astonishing recovery; I would say he has over-recovered, for now he comes right back with more of the same, in the same tone as before, muted now, perhaps, but still brass-edged. That he should already be capable of being precisely himself seems horrifying to me, but the grandmother, I realize, understood much better than I that this would be the case. She is having a first-class morning.

The cigar man, who has been staring at me off and on, sharply says to me, 'That your hand?' He jigs his chin downward; his jowl is squeezed outward, like a trumpeter's lip on a high note.

I see a blush scramble up Maisie's neck.

I do not think I should answer. I think perhaps I

should say something to the painter behind me, speaking over my right shoulder, and so presenting the back of my head to the cigar man, who already, worse luck, has had the back of my hand.

But Maisie, coming to my rescue, says to Havana, 'I asked him to put his hands on my hips. I was very frightened.'

'Oh,' says Havana, and swallows. He really must have thought she had been cozying up to him. Now *he* blushes.

Once when I was small my father spanked me with a felt bedroom slipper. What had I done to provoke him? It is the only memory I have of punishment at his hand, and it strikes me as a sad small parable of correction that I cannot even remember the crime for which I was paying a penalty. What I do remember is that the slipper was soft. I made the costly error of giggling. My father dropped the slipper and reached to the bureau top for a hairbrush, the back of which, I soon learned, was not soft.

'Want to know something funny?' I say to Havana. 'You remind me of my father. That is, you do and you don't.'

His blush deepens. Then he says in a manly voice, 'How old do you think I *am*?'

134

'I mean,' I say, 'the way I remember him when I was a kid.'

This helps very little. Havana turns his head away.

Lottery moves to the upper step and Maisie rises up on the lower one—and almost exactly with her, Havana steps up on one side of her and the teacher on the other. It is a convenient time for me to recover my hands. I am tempted to set my lips to the vulnerable in-curving place at the nape of Maisie's neck, but I have the sense not to. I do whisper directly into her ear, 'Thank you for what you said.'

She turns her head to the right and whispers, 'You mean to Daddy?'

I groan out loud, and she laughs.

I do want to speak to the painter. These hours in the line have been like a voyage. I have made one friend I want to see again, but the others, the painter among them, will have come into my life and gone out of it again forever, like fellow passengers briefly encountered on travels. Before the painter vanishes that way, I want to thank him for his common sense, to which we all owe our sanity, and, yes, for his crankiness, to which he probably owes his. He will be hostile to gratitude. He follows two crafts, he has no time for pleasantries. Keep moving! Keep it going! I respect his misanthropic urgency, and in

135

the end I decide I have no words to say to him that won't just waste his time.

The janitor—the survivor—is busy trying to persuade everyone around him to put in a word for him at the windows, to say that it was his leadership of the song that saved the waitline. He has already rearranged history, dropping from the record the inconvenient fact that it was really the painter's cool, contrary head that saved us. The janitor takes his revisionism so far as to ask the painter himself to put in a good word.

The painter just says, 'Look, friend. I have problems of my own.'

Maisie climbs the second step; I, the first. Taking this first rise under pressure is most awkward. I wedge my left knee between Maisie's left leg and the cigar man's right leg, but because of the crowding I cannot properly shift my weight to the left, and I am canted forward before I am ready to go up. Nevertheless, I push down with my left leg and rise in good order, in my narrow chute of touchers.

After a time Lottery is let through the police barrier and Maisie moves against it, and I rise onto the upper step. The barrier seems to be (I cannot quite see it, only sense it from what has been happening) a waist-high railing, in which, I gather, there are hinged gates, each

136

manned by a policeman. Beyond the railing is a space of about three feet on the upper landing before the doors, where there is much awkward jostling as the petitioners who are let through shove past the policemen and into the building.

I take a chance and say out loud to Maisie, 'Don't forget to wait for me.'

Once more she answers with a nod.

'Off to the right, okay?'

Another nod.

Then, before I can fetch out any more of the disorderly stock of things I want to say to her, she goes through. The back of her dress is dark blue from her sweat and mine. The wet cloth clings to her buttocks, and to the curving small of her back. I see a flash of her, full-length, as she pushes a swinging door in one of the arches. I have a fleeting hope that she will turn and look back, and I will see her whole face, but of course she does not. I would not say that her body from a rear view is sensational, but I realize that the big stain of our shared warmth on her back is not flattering.

She is gone. I am against the railing.

THE RAILING is greasy with the wipings of a decade of anxious palms. The officer in front of me is a harassed man who looks to be, as so many of New Haven's policemen are, of Italian descent. His dark cheek glistens, he has not been shaving that chin for many years. He frowns and lets fly with his elbows on passing petitioners as they crowd through the gate, but he gives instructions in the meticulously courteous tones I heard earlier, his cop's dress-uniform voice.

Now that the railing is cutting into my gut, the wait seems interminable. Maybe my sense that time has gone into an appalling stretch-out comes from the fact that Maisie is no longer in front of me. In a rush of fear that I will be separated from her after our petitions have been denied, I try to remember her address, and my fear grows into panic. I have forgotten it. It is on Park Street, that much I remember. Wasn't it a round number? 320? 410? There must be ten thousand people living in the span on Park between 320 and 410. I can't search every sleeping-hall. She knows I'm in the Marinson Building, but if we miss each other here, would she try to reach me, expecting, as she would, that I would get in touch with her?

I remind myself that she nodded when I asked her to wait for me; she will be there.

The grandmother knows the policeman in front of her from previous encounters at the railing. She calls him by his first name, Frank. He greets her with a warmth that may be feigned; understandably he cannot remember her name, and he calls her 'Mrs.'

The janitor is asking *his* policeman if there have been any hitches inside the building this morning.

'What you mean, hitches?'

'You know, disturbances, or like some son of a bitch asks for more space?'

'Don't know, sir,' the policeman says in his dark blue voice. 'You'd have to ask inside.'

This last flare-up of the janitor's hostility to me seems strangely smoky and wavering. He does not swing his nasal cleaver toward me, does not look at me with those close-set charcoals. He has asked the question as if it stemmed from some blurred memory of the distant past.

'Listen,' he is now urgently saying to the policeman. 'You heard those screams a while ago, right? You heard the singing, right? Listen . . .' And he tries to persuade the policeman to go inside with him and vouch at the windows for his role in stemming a disaster. All the while the cop is saying things over the janitor's head in his official voice, 'Take it easy, there . . . Don't push . . . You'll get in . . .'

I SEE THAT there is a system of signal lights attached to the rail. A blue bulb flickers near my left hand, and the grandmother's policeman, Frank, raises the bar in front of her.

Over her shoulder she says one last party farewell. 'Bye, Harry. Look me up, now.' And goes through. She squeezes past her uniformed friend, saying, 'See you, Frank.'

He suddenly drops his parade voice and says with a strange vehemence, 'I believe you will.' Then he turns back to watch the light again, shaking his head without compassion. What it must be like to have his duty day after day after day!

The janitor's light and mine flash at almost the same moment. Our bars go up. The impatience of the petitioners behind me propels me through the narrow opening, which tears at both my hips, and bumping past my man in blue I am impressed by the great strength of these barrier cops. Mine claps down the bar behind and against

140

my back with a weight-lifter's arm, holding the painter, and all the surge of hopes in back of him, in check. I crowd past the policeman into the archway slightly to my right and going through the doorway jostle the janitor—and I find *his* frame, after the running-guard meatiness of the cop's, light, delicate, fragile, as if his bones are hollow like a bird's. I feel that I may break his bitterness in two. I do believe he is hungry. I hold to our deal and run to the left inside the door, along a row of metal-pipe turnstiles at which petitioners are waiting. The fourth turnstile from the left is free. I duck into it.

After five hours of sardinehood, I feel, now, in this space, as large and free as a shark. I can almost see why the grandmother is hooked on petitions. One has slowly built to this sudden incredible high.

The ceiling, like my whirling brain, is also high—an ancient stamped-tinware affair, a curio of a ceiling, crusty with generations of layers of paint. The light, after the brilliance outside, is crepuscular, and for a moment I see a flickering dream-picture of myself in ecstatic twilight flight along the shoulder of West Rock. This is that same light from the center of a drop of amber, from the center of a sexual wish. The petition windows stand in a varnished mahogany bulkhead, with heavy carved-leaf moldings. The spirit of the distant past in the room, with

141

its signs of lavish, painstaking handcrafts, speaks a bitter irony, when one considers the sorts of scraps of life-left-overs the citizens streaming past these turnstiles beg for at the blank, faceless windows. These are just as Maisie described them. Bars; then opalescent empty glass. Have you ever looked into the eyes of sixteen blind men standing side by side?

I see Maisie. She is about five windows down to the right. The weight of her body is on one leg; the other leg, knee cocked, crosses inward; her hips are revolved a half turn on their sweet axis. Her dress still clings to her back. From here she looks all right. She is using her hands to argue; she knows that the window is not, after all, blind.

The cigar man is straight ahead of me. The back of his neck is scarlet over the black lapel of his synthetic-fabric suit coat.

I see the lottery man leave, walking to the right. He is crestfallen. His unshaven cheeks sag. He was surely entitled to more time at a window than he has taken. He is a person who lacks conviction, gives up easily, walks away hanging his head and muttering. Another day he'll think of another hopeless scheme.

The teacher is off to the right. Her manner is listless. Her towering panic has torn the roof off her habit of dis-

142

approval; her life is like a ruined house. What *was* it she could not wait to reach the windows to beg for?

And there is the grandmother, laughing hard at her window. She is having a beautiful high today. She does not really care whether little Robert learns to read. Relatives are a convenience to her; for fun she plays a table game in which the counters are her needs and theirs.

At the left and right ends of the line of turnstiles pairs of policemen sit at consoles, moving their hands like organists. They evidently control the turnstiles with switches; I presume they have some mechanism that keeps track of turns. When a petitioner wheels, bewildered, from his window, looks for exit, and walks dejectedly away, a turnstile here or there in the row clicks open, and one more excited, pent-up, sweat-wet creature hurries to the free place.

A<small>T ONE OF THE WINDOWS</small> to my right, two slots this side of Maisie's, a man is suddenly shouting and waving his arms, like someone trying to warn a friend of danger coming—but no, he is both angry and afraid; he looks more like a receiver than a giver of warnings. Looking for help, he turns his head to right and left, and when his face shows on my side his mouth loops around its goose-honk noise like the tightened mouth of a dufflebag. He is facing straight ahead again, still roaring, and now he has the audacity to beat his fists on the bars of the window before him. I hear pounding feet—and an echo of pounding feet—in this box of a room with an old metal ceiling; two policemen come running from off to the right. They grasp the shouting man by both his arms, and they drag him away; he howls like a moonstruck dog. The officers take the man to the street exit at the far end of the room, and they throw him out.

Now—CLICK!—BEFORE I have time to digest the fierce short drama I have just watched, my turnstile opens, and I am a racehorse let loose from its gate.

There is a free window to my right. I run forward fearful that someone else will leap from nowhere into the empty slot before me. As I rush toward it I realize that this is the window from which the shouting man has just been torn away. Does that matter? I have been waiting so long! I stand at last before the bars, the glass. Maisie is now two windows to my right. The teacher is next to me

144

on my left. The petitioner between Maisie and me is the bald man with the liver spots and maple-burl nose.

My distractions now, at a moment when I want to aim my entire being in a laser beam of supplication, are perverse and may be expensive. Off at a rough edge of attention I hear Maisie's voice raised in protest. All morning she and I have whispered or murmured to each other, and now to hear her contentious stridency is unsettling. This shouting Maisie is a stranger to me. She is a scold. The grandmother must have been right about Maisie's chances; she seems to be faring poorly.

Repeatedly I hear the voice/voices from behind the nearby windows, exactly as Maisie had described it/them—they are mincing, pinched, legalistic. It/they sounds/sound like/like echo/echoes.

'Name?' ('Name?')

I am aware that the janitor has moved up to the window just beyond Maisie's, and it strikes me as funny that, after all, he is so near to me. I had to move to the right from my turnstile to reach an empty window; he had to move to the left. Has he seen me?

The glass behind the bars has an iridescent quality, which I try to penetrate with imagination. Is a gnome-like man sitting beyond that shot-silk pane, with thin lips and thin hair, a very high forehead, wire-rimmed specta-

145

cles, a grasshopper body containing an immense negative power?

'Name?'

It *is* a rather mechanical sound, insistent and penetrating—and it finally cuts into my unfocused mind as
the voice behind my own window! I am startled and I
answer.

'Samuel D. Poynter.'

'D for?'

'Dead.'

'Levity is not permitted at this particular bureau.'

'I'm sorry. It's been a long morning. D for David.'
Who, I always say to myself, slew Goliath.

'Address.'

'524 Whitney Avenue. Marinson Building. Entry
Four.'

'Age.'

'Going on thirty-eight.'

'You are thirty-seven?'

'I am thirty-seven.'

'Give accurate answers.'

'I did. My birthday is less than a month away.'

I am getting off on the wrong foot. I came here to
make a dignified request, not to crack nits between my fin-
gernails.

146

The liver-spot man's voice trembles. The teacher is weeping.

On the mahogany panel above the window there is a high relief of a draped garland of leaves of ivy and holly, exquisitely worked in reddish wood. Looking up, trying to pull myself together, I visualize callused hands holding a mallet and a chisel to carve those leaves. Did the woodcarver love his work, or did the monotony of it overcome him? Each of the sixteen windows has such a garland, and the higher moldings I saw earlier are of the same pattern. Did the craftsman live with excruciating boredom—leaf after leaf after leaf of ivy and holly, season upon season of endless and changeless foliation? The dust and crud of many years have settled in the crevices—a mealy-bug of time and indifference on the delicate leaves. Who cares about the carver's patience now?

Who will ever care how much space I have? Who will ever wonder whether a writer of departmental reports loved his work?

I am aware that a question has been asked, or at least that a statement has been demanded of me. The gnome-like man of my imagination wishes to know what my petition is. Nestled deep among my distractions is the thin-voiced command that has just been uttered: 'State your petition.'

147

What the hell, shall I change my petition to something else—to some idiot nothing that no authority could begrudge me? I am suffocated by a sense of the futility of asking for what I need and want most in this world. They will think I have come here only to mock them, and, alas, they may be right.

The voice speaks without emotion: 'You are wasting other people's time.'

'First I want to give you some background. I am a writer——'

'Which department?'

I don't like that. Right away there is an assumption that I merely write departmental reports. The fact that I merely do is irrelevant. I am a writer——

'State your petition.'

There is a certain kind of stubbornness—I face it at this moment—which locks me into its reciprocal: elusiveness. When I hear this flat, droning, obsessive, repetitive note in the voice of someone who has no give, I go slippery. There is no use my telling myself that I am the one here who wants something.

'It is true that at the moment I merely write departmental reports. But that is not the point——'

'You are not the best judge of what the point is. Or is not.'

148

'If I may say so, the point is that the situation may change.'

Everything has changed within my lifetime—that is precisely what is so hard to accept. The day after a blizzard, once, when I was very small, my father hired a horse-drawn sleigh from a livery stable in Bethany. We drove out to the stable from New Haven on our snow tires; there were still privately owned vehicles in those days. By then horses were a flaming curiosity, the sleigh a money-making nostalgia-stunt. I remember my bliss that day—being tucked against my mother under a fur rug, the shiny brown haunches rising and falling before my eyes, the creaking of the runners on the snow. Miles and miles of just us three, and our driver made four, feathering the country air with the words we spoke. Bethany is now paved with concrete and asphalt very nearly from town line to town line; the last American horse was eaten before I was thirty.

Yet perhaps it can also be said that nothing has really changed. There is only more. What is hard to accept is the lack of change *within* the change.

'There is no law saying I have to write departmental reports all my life. I——'

'If your petition is to change jobs——'

'But it isn't.' These bureau people have kept me

149

waiting all morning, and now I'm going to keep this one at my window waiting awhile. 'To judge my petition you have to know me. I was born——'

'I already know you. "Poynter, Samuel David. Born New Haven Hospital by Caesarian section" etcetera etcetera etcetera.'

Oh God, of course these bureaucrats have access to the biobank; he must have punched out my name on a console as soon as I gave it to him. I can see myself all laid out in a rectangle of computer capitals; my entire existence is displayed on the dark field of a monitor, to one side of the bureau person's window, as a meager system of squarish characters of laminated layers of light.

'But there are some things that don't show up on there,' I say with some energy. 'I'll give you just one example of my mother's kindness. I mean, it wasn't a busybody thing—it was built in, and totally innocent. And, you know, it's part of me. This was back when we lived in a private room on Howe Street. A repairman came one day—the broiler element in our oven had burned out, and——'

'State your petition.'

What chills me is the uniformity of tone. There is no impatience, no force of feeling in this repetition of the command.

150

'The statute book states that your bureau is required to give a fair hearing to every petition. I don't think——'

'When our bureau has been informed what your petition is, it will give you a fair hearing on it.'

'You know something? I don't think I've been able to finish a single——'

'State your petition.'

Maisie is still talking in a loud, angry voice, and now Liverspots has begun to tune up into a whine. I cannot sift out from the general hubbub the sound of the janitor's words, beyond the racket Maisie is making, but I will wager he is already desperate.

If I am honest with myself, I cannot say that I have had a bad morning in conditions of minimal space. The pleasures of discovery, of having one's small wagers of self-confidence pay off, and of sharing what has seemed to be a secret—these still steady me; and Maisie's complaisance, her breaking of the law along with mine, her knack of tilting her head back toward me to express appreciation—her traits and moves, as much as my own temperament, have given me the patience to deal now with the glass voice beyond the glass.

'My petition'—I may as well come out with it—'is for more space.'

The building does not crash about my ears. The janitor is not driven howling from the windows. There is a slight pause, but there is no more emotion in the silence than there has been in the repetitions.

Then the voice says, 'What kind of space? Space in which to do what?'

I never expected such questions as these. I expected: *Why? Why you? Why are you entitled to more than the next person?*

I lamely bring in a literal answer. 'Space in the sleeping-hall.'

'For what purpose?'

For several months, some years ago, I did deep-breathing exercises. I forget now the theoretical basis for this gulping of air. There was some fourth-hand Yoga thrust to it. I was in a health phase: Tingling of the soma, quiet in the mind. *In one . . . two . . . three . . . four . . . five . . . six . . . seven out.* I remember the count of seven. It all went out in a rush. It was bad air, anyway. The rib cage was stretched to its limits. One vaguely guessed that one felt unworldly at least for the count of seven.

'Purpose? Space where I can breathe deeply.'

'Don't you breathe in the space you have? Marinson, Entry Four?'

Yes, I hear the note of sarcasm. The Marinson—well

known to be one of the buildings in New Haven that is
not bad to live in. The same flat tone as before; the jibe is
almost hidden. But I hear it, and hearing it is like going
through a door. I enter a new chamber of this interview.
I begin to understand the nature of the test. I must learn
from the whole texture of sound around me. I must admit
no anger, no whine, no haste, no weeping. My petition
may be the only important one that has ever been made
at these windows.

6

WHAT CAN ONE person do alone? My mother, who thought that humanity was perfectible, gave herself to a life of committees for improvement. There were certain committees she had to join, some in my sick father's stead—our obligatory committee of fifteen, our block committee, an endless train of school committees; but she also volunteered for many, many others. I remember the often-repeated scene—like a

sharply defined episode in a recurring dream—of her return to our Howe Street room from the meetings of these
groups. The door would fly open and its foot would crash
against the rubber-tipped doorstop beside the stove; the
whole door would creak in protest. Mother would be
standing in the doorway, a bag of groceries under an
arm—one unfathomable bluejay look at Father, one at
me. Not a word. Outwardly she was as serene as ever. In
she came and over-carefully closed the door, leaned back
against it a moment, took one resolute step forward, set
the groceries gently down on the stove top, and moved
toward the wall closet. She lifted a hand to the back of
her neck to unzip her committee dress. Zip! She had a
strange way of parting her teeth and sucking her lips into
her mouth, so she would get no lipstick on her dress as
she lifted it off over her head. When she grasped her
dress cross-armed at the hips and raised it to curtain her
face, her eyes were dry; by the time the hem rose above
her head, a torrent of tears was pouring from them. That
grotesque, old-womanish, wet, hollow-cheeked, sucking
grimace, under the canopy of cloth held high by bare
arms, was to me, and still remains, her most honest, and
yes, somehow, her most beautiful countenance—the face
she was obliged to make at human truth.

Later she would talk in subdued tones, in sadness

rather than malice, never about agenda, actions, substance, or lack of them, but always about this one's vanity, that one's galloping tongue, and another's drive for power, and later still she would gaze into my face with a look of appalling melancholy, which has haunted me ever since her death. In that gaze, the taproot of my pessimism.

I SAY, 'Through part of my childhood and all of my adolescence, my father was ill. I was alone with him a great deal. His patience and courage were my bread and milk. If he had had a gift for generalization, he would have been a philosopher.'

The voice must be reading from the monitor: 'Parkinsonism, sequel of *encephalitis lethargica* . . .'

Again it is the same tone, which says, We have this information already, this is nothing new to us—and mind you, within our infinite patience we have a little room for impatience with certain types of persons.

'Yes,' I say, adopting a new tone of my own, halfway between those of friendly intimacy and the indulgence one might grant a small child. 'Yes, his hands trembled, and he walked with a peculiar gait, knees slightly bent—

157

he *shuffled*. This was my father, you understand, the figure I was supposed to want to be like.'

'What has that to do with space?'

'I think he knew every line of Wordsworth by heart.'

'I remind you: Petitions have a definite time allowance.'

Every utterance from behind the glass is designed to throw one off balance. I realize that a determination to be calm ruffles the surface of the calm.

I ask, 'Are you listening to me?'

'With some difficulty.' Suggesting that even a bureau person has a right to rudeness.

'Try to follow me. He also liked Hardy—the poetry, not the prose. I thought it a strange combination, Wordsworth and Hardy.'

'You are eating up your time.'

'My father had space. His sickness tried to pin him down, but he was strong and he made space for himself.'

'So go make space for yourself.' It *is* listening. This answer was abrupt! Does the bureau after all have a skin that it is possible to get under?

'That was a' quarter of a century ago. There was space to make space in then. It's different now.'

'All spaces in the Marinson sleeping-hall are of equal size.' A shift. Yes, we have come to the expected challenge. Why should I, rather than the next person, have more space?

'You're wrong. There are three different sizes.' Single, married, married with child.

There is a pause. One can guess that the bureau does not relish being picked up on technicalities; that is the bureau's own game. 'All the spaces for single persons are of equal size. What do you say to that?'

I have waited for nearly four hours for this interview, and during that time . . . But something has changed in the texture of sound. I can hear the janitor's voice, going now like a crosscut saw. This means—of course!—that Maisie's voice is no longer a barrier. Has her time run out? Has her petition been denied? Has she left her window? I turn and look. No, she is still there. Her face is as white as a grocery bill. I am looking at the left—the humorous, the somewhat mischievous—profile of her face; the mouth is drawn down, that attractive bump above it no longer seems the gather of a half-smile. Her head is motionless, while beyond it the janitor's rides up and down with his arguments like the head of a galloping horse.

I feel anger on Maisie's behalf. Her petition is so benign. She wants no more than the sense of self-esteem, of superiority at worst, that would come from helping the

159

walking wounded. The bureau has put her through an ordeal of anger and, now, of blood-drained humiliation. The time has come for me to present the argument that *I am special*, but my flash of anger, which is a restless afterglow of my emotion and my erection in the line, derails me, and I merely say, 'The space for singles at the Marinson is forty-eight square inches less than the median of all single spaces in the city of New Haven.'

I know what the answer will be: That like any other citizen I should be aware that space allotments vary inversely with the quality of the accommodations—and anyway I haven't answered the question that had been implied: Why should a unique exception be made in my favor?

But this is not, as it turns out, the window's next response. Instead the voice says, 'Your labor duty was extended six months, it says here, because of quarrelsomeness. Are you having quarrels with holders of adjacent spaces?'

'I was assaulted that time.'

'Why?'

'I dumped some concrete on a man's foot. It was an accident.'

I have often wondered whether it was. The controls for guiding the chute to the forms were accurate and firm,

160

and that one spill was the only one I ever let fall. Did I, in the back of my head, at the moment I tugged at the release of that load, know that I wanted to find some roundabout way to try my friend's girlfriend?

I pull myself away from these rapid thoughts. I am on the defensive. I am encountering precisely the mechanism Maisie warned me against in the waitline, when she told me that the bureau, by its abrupt shifts and by the most subtle indirection, had, each time she had gone to the windows, undermined her belief in the moral base of her petitions.

Above the buzz and the clicking of the turnstiles and the echo effect of the bureau voice/voices, I hear a guffaw—the grandmother's hearty bellow. What a good time the old Tartar is having! She doesn't care. I pull her laughter around me, wanting to be enveloped by her indifference.

I need some not-caring as a shield for my caring.

My window asks, 'Why are you in a single space?'
In chess, my father did manage to teach me, when your opponent moves his knight you must look beyond the threat which that move in itself suggests and work out what future danger there may be, as a consequence

161

of the move, from the bishop far across the board, the castled rook, the innocent-looking pawn screening the queen.

I could reply: Because my wife and I are separated. But I imagine something is coming about my responsibility to my daughter. I decide not to commit myself, to keep my future moves flexible, and I say, 'Because I am classified in the registry at Orange Street as a single person.'

'It says here that fourteen years ago there were no less than sixteen faultily prepared application forms for permission to have a child.'

'The seventeenth form was deemed correctly filled out.'

'Ah,' the voice says. 'In November and December of last year and January of this year'—now the voice pauses, allowing me to wonder what is coming next. It has dropped the line about my daughter before really taking it up; the work of planting doubt on that score has been done. That castled rook can wait, lurk.

'—yes, *and* January of this year, your monthly reports were late, and printout warnings were issued by the computer.'

I am suddenly furious. I fight my anger bravely, as my father fought his *paralysis agitans*, but his hands

162

shook with the effort, and so does my voice now. 'I don't call this a fair hearing on my petition. You're just trying to impeach my character.'

'Very good,' the voice says—and means it. 'You were telling us why Samuel David Poynter, alone of all the people in Marinson Entry Four sleeping-hall, should have his space enlarged. By the way, how much enlargement did you have in mind?'

The voice this time has allowed itself some expression. The last question had unmistakable inflections of irony—of a very heavy sort, bespeaking the dull metal embedded in that word.

This tone puts me on more solid ground, and I say with composure, 'I request a space eight feet by twelve.'

'Single allotments in the Marinson are——?'

'Seven by eleven.'

'Our question was: How much enlargement did you——'

'I am requesting nineteen additional square feet.'

'A space one foot wider and one foot longer would satisfy your needs?'

'No. Eight by twelve is the maximum allowable by law for singles.'

'But you think a space one foot wider and one foot longer would change the quality of your life?'

163

'Definitely.'

'Has it occurred to you that your being granted this petition would mean that another single person would lose more than one-fifth of his or her allotment?'

'There are other ways . . .' I have worked out several plans for stealing space from neutral areas, but the petition-window is apparently not interested.

It says, 'How would this change your life?'

This is a tease. Holding out possibility like a dog bone for me to gnaw on—asking me to speak of the effect on me of a (possible?) granting of my petition. Should I sit up and beg? . . . No! I must get the initiative back. Right now the voice is making all the pressing moves. I am special. My petition is special. I must not let myself be drawn into humdrum traps. I must not go the humble route of Maisie, Liverspots, the teacher, the lottery man walking out with a hanging head.

I often have a dream of getting lost. We are near the labor camp. The day's work is done. Some kind of social event has been planned, and I have an important role to play—I am to give a lecture in Italian. I have not prepared it. In fact I do not know Italian, except in gestures. I am in a great hurry to get back in time to prepare myself. There will be a sensuous reward if I do well, a terrible, bleak feeling of loss if I do not. I run through a land-

164

scape of buildings under construction—sometimes I am in trenches dug for foundations, I climb over wooden forms for concrete, I run along behind a moving crane on caterpillar-tracks, and here is a great field of rubble of knocked-down buildings. The former gymnasium is somewhere ahead, beyond a hill of half-walls and chimney stumps. *There is not a single human being anywhere*, not even in the cab of the moving crane. The footing is loose. My legs ache. It is almost time for the lecture. I have forgotten where it is to be held. I can hardly lift one thigh after the other. But I run! I run! . . .

'If only I had more space,' I hear myself saying, 'I would have more time.'

'How's that again?'

'My reports were late in the three months you mentioned—and they've been late in other months, too—because I wanted them to catch somebody's eye. At first I tried to accomplish that by giving them a certain elegance—elegance, I mean, of proof, of the sort mathematicians speak of. I think I partly succeeded. But nothing. No attention. As far as I know, nobody read them. Then I got the idea of turning them in late. If I did this several months in a row, perhaps somebody besides the computer would wonder . . . would read . . . '

'This was not good for your department.'

'How many petitions do you handle a day?'

'At one window, or altogether at the bureau?'

'At *your* window.'

I say this as if there is in fact behind this window a light-bodied man with a domed forehead, wire-rimmed spectacles . . .

'Fifty. More or less.'

'Six days a week?'

'What has this to do with Marinson Entry Four?'

'Everything. Multiply this by sixteen windows. Eight hundred petitions a day. Nearly five thousand a week. No wonder the bureau hates petitioners.'

'The bureau has no feeling about petitioners one way or another.' The voice, I must say, bears out this assertion.

'Exactly. You couldn't care less. . . . Look, there must be three or four thousand people out there in the waitline. It goes around the corner and God knows how far down Elm Street. This is the sixth morning in a row I've waited to get to this window.'

'And what has this to do with——'

Now I feel that I do have the initiative, and I switch the line. 'My wife couldn't have sexual pleasure with people watching.'

There is a pause. Then: 'Could you imagine it possi-

166

ble that something about you may have been the reason
she——'

'I could, and if something about me *was* the reason
for her trouble, I'd put my bottom dollar on it that my relationship to space was that something.'

'Nineteen more square feet equals sexual fulfill-
ment?'

If only I could *see* the slight-bodied figure behind
the glass! . . . My naked wife went limp and wept at the
unreal—yet also real—thought of the many eyes . . . I
wanted eyes—many or few, or even two—to see the marks
I made on paper. . . . This oily glass in the amber light
blocks the primary sense—the sense which, more than all
the others, defines space, gives lips and breasts and
thighs reality and literature its power. And guides human judgment—for eyes look into eyes to find the elusive
truth that spoken words so often blur. The window's
glass renders that kind of truth-seeking impossible here.
This is what makes authority so infuriating: It always
hides its eyes.

I SAY, 'No, you're on the wrong track. Space and
time for sex are only part of what I mean. How long do

167

you think citizens are going to accept the Acceptance slogans?'

'Are you suggesting——'

'I'm not suggesting anything. I am arguing a petition.'

I have heard a tiny hint of fear and rage in the epicene counsellor's voice behind the window. Yes, my petition *is* a frightening one. It frightens even me. The fantasy of being so deep in an ancient forest that if I shouted with all my might I would not be heard by a single human ear fills me with a delicious terror. But the potential for panic in the voice behind the glass is not in dreamed-of woods; it is out there on Church Street.

'Did you hear the shouting in the waitline about half an hour ago?'

'We could hear the noise—but not the words.'

'A man next to me called out to the people in the line to tell them what my petition was going to be. He roused them up pretty well.'

'Do you know the penalties for incitement?'

'I was not inciting. I was being incited against.'

My heart is beating fast. I am trying as hard as I can, like a tiring boxer, to keep out of range of the blows that come at me through this vague amber light, to dodge, to

168

counterpunch the moment I sense a lowered guard, but all the while, on another level, I can hear the crowd shouting, 'Out! . . . Out! . . . Out! . . .' My outrage, my protest—not at all popular. In the shadows of my mind, the janitor pumps his arms, and there is a look of malicious joy on his weak-chinned face. Or are those the arms of the woodcarver of the garlands over my head? He holds the chisel, he swings the mallet, and he knows the grain of the wood, he knows of the years of sunshine that went into the wood, the years of leaves going sere and drifting down to rot on the ground, unnoticed.

'You told others that you were planning to enter a petition for more space?'

I am feeling irritable. Who cares about the wood-carver's patience? Not I! Who will ever care what I put in my reports?—or what my petition one day was?—or how deeply I could or could not breathe? My voice, when I speak, crackles with strong feeling. 'Everybody tells everybody. There's time to talk out there in the waitline, did you know that?'

'Well, then'—the mechanical voice from behind the window pings again with the sound of assurance, doubt-less because I have let myself slip into anger—'you were inciting.'

'Just to talk about——'

I break off. I feel that it is time to take one of those deep Yoga breaths.

Inhaling, I am aware that the grandmother is leaving in a whirlwind of jaunty exclamations to people waiting at the turnstiles and slightly mocking farewells to the backs of others pleading at the windows. If her petition has been turned down, as she assumed it would be, with her lore that all are, she is still able to be proud that Robert has been selected from all the thousands of city pupils to learn to read. It has been a super morning in her life. Many new friends; fainted woman hand-passed right over her head; darling man behind her stabbed by the icepick fear of line-sickness; the teacher, too—so close by; and then the lullaby. She moves behind me from my left to my right, indiscriminately wishing people luck. Lack of discrimination is just as much a form of hatred as lack of feeling; I guess I must face it that this jolly grandmother hates everybody. Her cheerful passage, at any rate, confirms my deep pessimism, for she is the one who kept telling us that petitions are never granted.

'Do you know,' my window is asking me, 'the penalties for incitement?'

'Do you know what your bureau is famous for?'

Again a pause. I can imagine a gleam of anxious cu-

170

riosity in the eyes (if there really *are* eyes) behind the wire-rimmed glasses behind the nacreous glass—but the bureau person surely does not want to admit wanting to know the answer to my question.

I offer it: 'Denial.'

This time the voice comes smartly back. 'Your time is nearly up. Say what you want to say.'

I HAVE STOPPED wearing a watch. It began to sicken me to think of the proportion of the remainder of my life that would be spent waiting. I am driven, anyway, to be punctual. My heartbeat tells me all too clearly when I am late, and I also have reason to know that the computer keeps track of my tardiness.

The voice has told me, as my heart also has, that it is time to say whatever it is I want to say.

I suddenly think, as I am trying to remember what it is I want to say: If my time is nearly up, Maisie's must already have expired. I look to the right. A stranger, a fat man with a sallow, shrewd face, has taken Liverspots' place; and at the next window the sighing black woman who was to the right of the painter in the line is now speaking with bulging eyes and a moist upper lip; and at

the window beyond hers, the janitor's nose no longer
rides his emphases. So Maisie has left the windows. I look
farther along the line; she agreed to wait for me off to the
right. I cannot see her.

'What I want to say——'

'You have exactly one minute.'

One minute! But that is ridiculous. 'I haven't even
begun to tell you——'

'Better begin.'

Beginning when I was twelve or thirteen years old,
and up until the very eve of my departure for labor duty,
part of me simply couldn't stand to be anywhere near my
parents. Their most gentle inquiries I rewarded with
snarls. Whenever friends of mine came to see me, and
my parents were in the room, I walked around with awkward heavy steps, as if a diver's suit of embarrassment
were tightly stretched over my skin. What seemed to be
on my mind, if I can recall it from this distance, was that
they had started me off in the world all wrong; they were
different from other parents, they had no understanding
of the world my friends and I lived in, and they were trying their best to make me be like themselves—different
from everyone else and, above all, different from my con-
temporaries. In other words, they wanted me to be special. One night as I was going to bed, I broke into tears

172

and began to pour all this out to them. They were
shocked and responded lovingly, at first gently belittling
my complaints, then blaming themselves and praising
me, and I, sensing their heartfelt consternation, seeing
what a splendid impression I was making on them, could
not resist going beyond the sincere feelings I'd been
venting up till then, and I began acting to the hilt the
role of a son ill-prepared for the world I luridly described, which they would never comprehend. Their agony fanned out like a glorious peacock's tail. I almost
laughed through my tears. . . . My summons to labor
duty, which was to tear me once and for all from their
arms, partly opened my eyes again to their love; but it
must have been two years later, one evening in our labor
battalion dormitory, that crowded gym, when my friend,
the one on whose foot I was eventually to drop the load
of cement, and whose girl in due course I took away, told
me, as we reminisced about younger years, of a scene in
which, at about the same age, he had dealt with his parents *exactly* as I had with mine—the same grievance, the
same tears, the same heightened drama, the same pleasure beneath the same pain; and I suddenly saw, much
too late to make decent amends to my sad mother and
my sick old father, that it was quite possible that I was
not as special as I had thought. . . .

173

A flicker of this memory cuts into what I have wanted to say, and what I *do* say is not what I have wanted to say at all, but is a hopelessly flat confirmation of my misgivings back then. What I say is, 'I've figured out a way of taking space away from neutral areas in the sleeping-hall, so no one else loses anything.'

This sentence is only halfway out when I hear its slightly whining, apologetic tone. I *must* not end on this note. The voice behind the window is silent; the bureau person apparently means to give me my full minute without interruption. Every time my heart beats, almost a second is forever lost.

It hits me very hard that a few minutes ago, after I said, 'If only I had more space, I would have more time,' and the voice asked me what I meant by that, I did not explain, but instead went on to talk about my idea that if my reports were late, then someone might read them.

So now I am finally responsive. 'When I said, "If only I had more space, I would have more time," this is what I meant: I spend so much physical and psychic energy pushing against people and limits that I am always too tired to do quickly the things I want and need to do.'

'True for everyone,' the voice replies with an alacrity that seems to say, I am not too tired to be quick, de-

spite the fact that what you have noticed is also true even
for a bureau person.

I suppose it is simply not enough to be the son of a
kind mother and a brave father; at this moment I am not
feeling at all special. The word from behind the window,
everyone, has shaken me. . . . Three heartbeats. Is this
minute going to last forever? It seems tensely stretched
out like the rubber bands of a slingshot. If time is indeed
space, this minute is as long as the Green, as deep as the
ancient forest which the whispering leaves on the trees
on the Green seem to remember. And I am lost in that
forest. I shout, but no human ear hears me.

I force myself to shout, 'A writer needs——'

'Nothing that a bus driver doesn't need.'

This time the voice has been excessively quick. Such
speed has a bad name: curtness. Why a bus driver? What
a strange choice! So many bus drivers are bad-tempered.
One can hardly blame them, but it is a fact. . . . And
suddenly I have lost *my* head, and I hear myself really
shouting now.

'You can't even let me have my last minute to say
what I want to say!'

'Say it, say it.'

But now I don't know what I want to say. I have

175

nothing to say. I am shouting something, but it is nothing. My arms are flailing—warning a friend of imminent danger? Do my angry gestures have anything to do with the words that fly out of my mouth?

The voice behind the window says, 'Your time is up. Petition denied.'

Now I distinctly hear the words I shout. 'This has not been a fair hearing. You haven't given me a chance to say what I want to say. You interrupt every time I start a sentence. . . . ' My shouts get louder and louder.

There is no expression at all in the voice as it says, 'Shall I call the officers?'

I have seen the athletic policemen smartly do their duty when called, and I remember that it was from this very window that they dragged that shouting man away. I do not answer out loud, but I shake my head to say, No.

'Good,' the voice behind the window says. 'Move along, please.'

I AM IN A DAZE as I walk away from the window. There is the painter—that sensible man—talking with *his* window quite reasonably, as far as I can tell. I have a stark impression of the drawn faces of the petitioners

176

waiting at the turnstiles. I search my heart in vain for disappointment; in fact I feel some slight push of elation—
but mostly I am embarrassed, like a schoolboy who has
given the wrong answer and has set the whole class
laughing. My face is hot; I am sure it is red. This has all
happened exactly as Maisie said it was going to happen.

Maisie! I expected to find her at the end of the room,
beyond the two uniformed organists playing their tune
of turnstiles; I thought she would be against the wall,
near the street door at the end of the hall, watching for
me, showing me for the first time her full face. She must
have been too depressed by her time at the window to
have wanted to stay any longer in this place; she must
have ducked outside; she will be waiting out there beside
the door, in the shadow of the archway. The street must
still be crowded at this hour, but there will be room for
her under the arch.

Last night I lay awake most of the night, going over
and over my expectations of this morning, without having been able to visualize anything so faceless as those
opalescent windows, and without ever having put into
words my yearning, my need. For some reason, even
though I had heard the expression 'petition windows,' I
pictured a room crowded with desklets, beside each one
a petitioner quietly talking with a visible bureau person.

I was full of hope. I was inflated by hope, I lay light on my bed lifted above sleep by hope.

Now as I hurry toward the street door, that hope having been let whooshingly out of me like compressed air from a tank, I am nevertheless full of hope all over again. My time at the window emptied me; pacing toward the door I am full again. One thought of that picture which I imagined earlier, of two people sitting on a bed, heels drumming on the wooden chest below, exchanging memories like traders bartering real goods, each trying not just to strike a bargain but really to get the best of the other—to gain those powers over the other that we sometimes call being a friend and being in love—one thought of that picture and I am as if I had not been at the window at all. In twenty paces I realize this, and I wonder: Did the space my father built around himself consist of his intimacy with my mother? Did Wordsworth and Hardy have anything to do with it? He used to speak their poems to her, I remember that.

There are two policemen at the door; they are the hearty ones who rushed that poor man out who had overstayed his time at my window. I nod pleasantly to them, one after the other. There is a metal lock-bar across the door, and I lean on it; it clatters, and the door swings

178

open. The amber light is diluted by a sudden pouring in of the clear day outdoors, and my dazzled eyes now see, as through a milky filter, a familiar reality: a teeming street.

I look to the right. No Maisie. I look to the left. No Maisie under the arch of the doorway.

For the pedestrians going toward Elm Street, there is a bottleneck here, caused by the waitline for the bureau building, which heads up to within a few feet of this archway. Quickly scanning the backed-up pool of these people who are trying to get to work, I hunt among their hats and scalps for a gather of swept-up hair. If Maisie is looking this way, I might not recognize her; I have not seen her face straight on. Was she swirled away from this doorway against her will by the current of humanity that slowly but inexorably flows off to the right?

I stand two steps above the pedestrians. I look off to the right over their heads, searching for Maisie's lifted hair, and I see the excited faces of those who are waiting to submit their petitions.

The door clanks open behind me and hits me in the back. It is the painter coming out. 'Fucking bureaucrats,' he growls, and he pushes past me.

I step down into the crowd and am taken into its tidal motion. We eddy very slowly toward Elm; at least we move. The sky is almost cloudless now, and the air has the heaviness of eyelids when one is falling asleep.

The siren hoots once.

'What time is that—nine fifteen?' I ask a man wearing dark glasses, on each lens of which I see a long-necked picture of me.

'Yup,' he says, and nods twice, and the two of me swoop up and down, my necks lengthening and shortening alarmingly as my heads and torsos rise and fall at varying rates of speed determined by the uneven convexities of the lenses.

These double enormities, made of me yet distorting me, throw me into a violent temper. My anger surprises me; it is not at these lying dark glasses, nor at the prissy-voiced grasshopper-man behind the window of shimmering light in there, nor is it at careless, faithless Maisie, nowhere to be seen. It is at the filthy computer. It tells on me when I am late. I could get my reports in on time if I wanted to. It is nine fifteen; I have planned my morning very well, and I have an hour and a quarter to get to my desklet, enough time if I push along; but I am tempted to be late. Let it tattle!

We have come to the head of the waitline, and it is

180

my lot to be forced to shuffle along next to the outer row
of the line—and rubbing shoulders hard with those who
are waiting I think of the janitor's complaint about the
wear and tear on his right arm, 'all futzed up' by pedestrians, and as I look at the faces of these people who have
almost reached the doors of the bureau building, and see
their feverish excitement, I remember my own swirling
emotions when I had reached this point in my long wait,
and suddenly I am pressed hard, from all sides, in both
my memory and my anger, by the grandmother and the
crusty painter and by that hungry survivor of a janitor,
and by Handlebars and the teacher and the seedy loop-
hole hunter with his pathetic lottery and the cigar man
flickering in moments of what seemed, then did not
seem, mimicry of my poor faltering father—and, with
nothing but hot wet cloth between us, by Maisie, who
seemed to understand me so well, damn her eyes, damn
her eyes. And while my anger still hovers around the
computer, an idea hits me—and once again I feel an in-
flow of hope, which does not dissolve my anger but rather
crystallizes it.

The idea is this: Perhaps I should enter a petition for
more time to write my reports. Yes, that idea has its appeal.

I could get my reports in on time if I wanted to. But if I had *more* time . . .

Not tomorrow. Perhaps the day after. That will give me a while to think through, more carefully than I did before this morning, what I will want to say at the petition window.

The people in this part of the waitline are chatting with great animation, doubtless asking each other what their petitions are. I see a golden tooth, a bouncing lip, a sexy eye.

Yes, maybe I will come the day after tomorrow and enter a petition for more time.

182

A Note about the Author and on the Type

JOHN HERSEY was born in Tientsin, China, in 1914, and lived there until 1925, when his family returned to the United States. He studied at Yale and at Clare College, Cambridge University. After serving for several months as secretary to Sinclair Lewis, he worked as a journalist and war correspondent. Since 1947 he has devoted his time mainly to fiction. He has won the Pulitzer Prize and is a member of the American Academy of Arts and Letters. From 1965 to 1970 he was Master of Pierson College at Yale, and he spent the following year as Writer-in-Residence at the American Academy in Rome. He now lives in New Haven, Connecticut, and teaches at Yale.

Hersey designed this book and set the text himself on the Yale Editor, New Haven, Connecticut, in a film version of CALEDONIA, a type face designed by W. A. Dwiggins. The book was printed and bound by The Haddon Craftsmen, Inc., Scranton, Pennsylvania.

Hersey
My petition for more space